Attack on Titan

LOST GIRLS

Created by Hajime Isayama
Stories by Hiroshi Seko
Art by Ayumu Kotake

Translated by
Maria Maita-Keppeler and Frank J/E Spinelli

 VERTICAL.

Art by Ayumu Kotake.

Originally published in Japanese as *Shousetsu Shingeki no Kyojin: LOST GIRLS*.
"Introduction" and "Lost in the Cruel World" translated by Maria Maita-Keppeler,
"Wall Sina, Goodbye" and "Lost Girls" translated by Frank J/E Spinelli.

This is a work of fiction.

ISBN: 978-1-942993-35-3

Manufactured in the United States of America

First Edition

Vertical, Inc.
451 Park Avenue South
7th Floor
New York, NY 10016
www.vertical-inc.com

CONTENTS

Introduction

I expect anyone who picks this book up without knowing the circumstances surrounding it will be quite surprised. It is easy to imagine how one might be confused as to the context in which this particular book exists. Were I in your position, I probably would be confused as well, and to a considerable degree at that.

Anyways, because of the special provenance of this book, I would like to borrow the space that we call an introduction to explain simply how it was completed.

Firstly, the two stories "Lost in the Cruel World" and "Wall Sina, Goodbye" were included in the bonus features of the third and sixth Blu-ray releases of the anime *Attack on Titan* as "visual novels." It is because an editor from Kodansha's Children's Literature Department wanted to compile these stories into a single volume that this work exists.

However, I felt somehow unsatisfied with making a book out of just the two stories "Lost in the Cruel World" and "Wall Sina, Goodbye," so in collecting them, I went ahead and composed the title story, "Lost Girls." Additionally, I took advantage of the opportunity to revise the first two stories.

The timeline of each of these stories coincides (maybe) with the original manga (and animation) as follows: "Lost in the Cruel World" with the manga's 7th episode (the anime's 7th), "Wall

Sina, Goodbye" with the 21st (the 16th), and "Lost Girls" with the 17th and 33rd (the 4th and 25th), respectively. Between the panels and the pages (or between the cuts and the scenes), each of these stories exists quietly, like a bookmark pressed in a novel sleeping in the back of a bookshelf.

As to why these are Mikasa and Annie's stories (why they necessarily tell of these two taciturn young women), there is a distinct reason. If I begin to explain it, however, it will become a very long story, so I will spare you the details. If I may say just a few words nevertheless as someone with a passing relationship to *Attack on Titan*, my interest (and heart) is hopelessly drawn to the burdens carried by Mikasa and Annie, and at the same time, *to the burdens they are probably carrying*, and I think I wanted to understand the young women on a deeper level by writing about them on my own.

Lastly (and perhaps superfluously), please allow me to make one practical addition. The alphabet makes an appearance in "Wall Sina, Goodbye." This doesn't mean that it is used in the world of *Attack on Titan*, but rather that it seemed a fitting contemporary representation for the writing system actually used in that world. The Japanese syllabary would have served as well—I simply adopted the alphabet to suit the tenor of the fictional world. I hope the reader understands.

October 2014
Hiroshi Seko

Lost in the Cruel World

1

It is raining. It is a rain so fine it is closer to fog. It is the kind of rain that makes it difficult to tell whether it is raining or not. It is a rain that is quiet, and cold, and without personality. It began just a little while ago, and since then has continued off and on. Mikasa doesn't much like rainfall; it is cold when it rains.

A boy kneels on one of the battered rooftops, his voice heavy with sobs. Mikasa knows the boy very well. His name is Armin. Armin Arlert—Eren's childhood friend.

Armin is calling out names.

"...Thomas Wagner, Nac Tius, Mylius Zeramuski..."

His voice blends into the sound of the quiet rainfall, and echoes as if from far away—very far away. Or perhaps, it is a voice delivered from the Outside World.

Long ago (to Mikasa, it truly seems like a far distant past), Eren often spoke to her about the Outside World. By the warm flames that danced in the fireplace on cold nights when everything was covered in frost, and on blistering, hot afternoons at the riverbank, where cool breezes blew, Eren spoke of the Outside World as if he were revealing some kind of precious secret.

In the Outside World there was something called "firewater."

LOST GIRLS

There was an "earth of ice," and a "snowfield of sand." There was something called the Sea that was made entirely of salt water. Such a world existed somewhere beyond the wall, and it was many times as vast as the one inside of it.

For the most part, Mikasa didn't care about the Outside World at all. Whether it was within the wall or beyond the wall, it didn't really matter. To her, what was important was whether or not Eren was beside her.

Whenever Eren spoke about the Outside World, however, he seemed so full of joy. Like some child playing innocently in a field on a beautiful, sunny afternoon, he seemed truly happy. Though seeing Eren like that filled Mikasa with warmth, at the same time she feared that this thing called the Outside World might some-day steal Eren and take him far away, farther than Mikasa's hands could ever reach. Those two feelings came and went as she listened to Eren talk.

Inside the wall, everything had been so peaceful. Whenever she returned to her home in Shiganshina, Uncle Grisha and Aunt Carla greeted her warmly. And always, Eren was beside her. But that was a long, long time ago.

"…Eren Yeager," Armin says. Suddenly, his voice stops.

Mikasa knows what is going to happen next. She hopes her prediction is wrong. Of course, she isn't wrong. Bad feelings always come true.

Armin continues, "Those five fulfilled their missions and were killed honorably in action."

Lost in the Cruel World

Mikasa steers her Vertical Maneuvering Equipment and soars through the rainy sky. She extends a steel cable and drops an anchor into the nape of a Titan's neck. Revving the machine, she reels in the wire. She tightens her grip on her sword, then slices off the nape of the Titan's neck. She slices it off perfectly.

It's easy, Mikasa thinks. So easy. Compared to the difficulty of protecting Eren, anything is easy.

The Titans are walking, their ominous footsteps thundering as they trudge onwards. They march as if they own the neighborhood, which has been turned into a battleground. Mikasa counts— one, two, three of them.

She extends a steel cable and drops an anchor into the nape of a Titan's neck. She revs her machine, then slices off the nape of its neck. She does this three more times. It is so easy.

For Mikasa, however, this repetition no longer holds any meaning; it no longer gets her anywhere. She would never get anywhere, no matter what she did. *Where am I trying to go?* Mikasa wonders. *Where is my destination?*

Out of the corner of her eye she sees a Titan—a ten-meter-class. It stares at her from the shadows of a building. Ribs jut out of the Titan's gaunt body, and yet a grotesque belly balloons out of its abdomen. Its arms are too long, its legs are too short, and its spine twists at an odd angle. It has the appearance of some kind of deformed frog, with an expression that is almost a smile pasted upon its face. The Titan's eyes squint out from above a bulbous nose, the two pupils looking off in different directions. Its right eye is locked onto Mikasa. The Titan stretches its long arm.

Mikasa revs the machine, changes her trajectory, and dodges the Titan's arm. Its nape is in plain view. She pierces her anchor into the back of its neck and revs the machine. Then she slices the nape cleanly off, soars up into the rainy sky, and speeds away.

Where? Mikasa wonders. *Where am I supposed to go?*

Suddenly the gas runs out. The Equipment gives a helpless whimper—*ploop*—and dies.

Eren is dead? It's a lie. It has to be a lie. It can't be. There's no way it could have happened. It isn't allowed to happen. Of all the things that could happen, that's the one thing that shouldn't have.

These thoughts circle through Mikasa's head as she falls.

Raindrops fall upon Mikasa's face. The wet sky stretches out before her eyes. It is a dull, gray sky.

Whew, Mikasa thinks. *I can't believe I didn't even realize I was out of gas.* She lies on a shop awning. The soft linen must have broken her fall. If she had fallen on the ground she certainly would have been killed. Good luck had come her way, or perhaps it was bad luck.

Either way, it is cold. The fine rain soaks through her coat and her pants and reaches down even into her scarf, underwear, and boots. The heat has left her previously burning body, and the cold now pierces her to her core.

It's never going to leave, Mikasa thinks. *I am going to have to live with this coldness for the rest of my life.*

"It's cold," Mikasa tries saying out loud. *Horribly cold. Since*

Lost in the Cruel World

when did it become so cold? It was so warm just a few moments ago.

Through her rain-blurred vision she sees something flying, something bright white. Mikasa blinks a few times and her vision becomes a little clearer. A butterfly flutters before her eyes, so white that it is almost transparent. So white she can see right through its wings to the other side. *A butterfly?* Mikasa thinks. *But this is a battleground.*

From far away she can hear screams, and groans, and sobs. She can also hear the *thump, thump* of the Titans' footsteps. The air smells of blood and rain. The walls of the buildings are smeared with blood. She can't see the ground; it is so thickly strewn with body parts and innards. Legless corpses are arranged on the ground like fragile figurines, still clutching their swords. Corpses that have been stepped on are plastered against the ground, bits of bone piercing through their skin. There are also many corpses that, for whatever reason, remain whole. Those who must have chosen to take their own lives slouch below the eaves of buildings, with their throats slit. Corpses of all different kinds are scattered over the ground. Several soldiers have dissolved into a muddy pulp that has clumped together into one pile. There are several of these piles. Hair and organs and flesh and pieces of bone and brains are mixed into pools of blood on the ground.

It is a scene that Mikasa has seen far more than she wanted on her way from the rear guard. She doesn't have to see any more to know: This is a battlefield.

Still, despite everything, the butterfly dances before Mikasa's eyes. It drifts between the blood-soaked land and the wet, gray sky.

It flutters aimlessly, elegantly. *It could have been caught and eaten by a praying mantis,* it suddenly occurs to Mikasa. She lifts her heavy arm and tries to grasp the butterfly. The butterfly apparently does not wish to be caught, however, and slips through her fingers. Mikasa lowers her hand.

The thick rainclouds droop low in the sky. Endlessly, they cast down the misty rain.

It's the rain's fault, Mikasa thinks. *It's all the rain's fault. Bad things always happen on rainy days. If that's the case, it might as well rain harder. It might as well rain more intensely, more savagely, and wash it all away. Every little thing.*

Mikasa closes her eyes. *Where did I go wrong? What did I do wrong? Why couldn't I protect Eren?* No matter how many times she repeats these questions, there is of course no answer. No matter how many questions pile up, they never amount to anything.

That's it, Mikasa thinks. *I made a mistake somewhere along the way, and that mistake has brought me here, to this rainy day. But if I could see Eren just once more—*

You need to stop this, she tells herself. *Don't think about anything anymore.*

2

When Mikasa awoke, it was raining outside her window. From the quiet sound of raindrops, and the dimness of the light streaming through the cracks in the curtains, she knew instantly that it was raining. Though the cold usually kept her from getting out of bed, she sprang up and opened the curtains. When she was sure that it was raining, she jumped in delight. Mikasa loved the rain.

Mikasa loved the rain because when it rained, Mother and Father stayed at home. On sunny or overcast days, Father would go out hunting, and Mother would take care of the garden, or do laundry, or clean—somehow she would be busy with work. But on rainy days both her parents stayed at home, and her family would gather around the dining table to do their jobs. Father would repair his hunting tools or prepare for lunch (on rainy days he always cooked lunch, and that lunch was always a little more extravagant than usual), and Mother would knit sweaters or gloves or scarves for Mikasa and Father, or bake goodies with flour and honey. Beside her parents, Mikasa would draw, or read picture books, or study reading and writing and math. Like that, from morning to evening, the three of them would spend the day together. The soft sound of raindrops on the roof, the smell of rain, the sight of the drizzle cloaking the forest outside the window, and the steady warmth that emanated from the fireplace—these things made Mikasa truly happy.

The mountain where Mikasa and her family lived rarely saw any rain, though. The last time it had rained was when Mikasa was only eight years old. For that reason, rainfall was something very precious to her.

That was why when Mikasa awoke that morning and realized it was raining, she felt as if she was being blessed by the world.

That day, while Father prepared lunch, Mother taught her embroidery. Though she had been taught how to knit and sew before, it was her first time learning how to embroider.

"This embroidery has been passed down in our family for generations," Mother said. "When you have your own children you will teach them as well."

Mikasa thought about what Mother had said for a moment before responding.

"How are children made?"

"Well..." Mother said with a somewhat troubled look on her face. "Why don't you ask your father?"

Mikasa looked at him.

"Hey, Father."

"Well now, I don't really know either," Father answered with an even more troubled expression. "It's almost time for Dr. Yeager to come—why don't you ask him?"

Right, Dr. Yeager was coming over for Mother's examination.

Lost in the Cruel World

Mikasa had completely forgotten. *What a waste of a rainy day*, Mikasa lamented. *If he was coming over anyways it might as well have been a sunny day.*

At that moment, as if to chide her selfish thoughts, there was a knock at the door—*tap, tap, tap*. It was a hard, dry, curt knock.

"Looks like he's here," Father said.

Tap, tap, tap—again the sound.

"Yes!" Father called and opened the front door. "Dr. Yeager, we've been expecting you. Please come in."

"Pardon the intrusion," said the man who entered the home, his entire body covered with a raincoat. He was about Father's age, tall, and wore glasses. His long, straight, black hair was tied in the back, and he carried a big black bag. Dr. Yeager.

"Hello, Mikasa," he said.

"Hello," Mikasa said, bowing her head. She had met Dr. Yeager a few times when she was still very young, but that was so many years ago, she hardly remembered him.

Dr. Yeager leaned out the door and called to somebody.

"Come on, Eren! Stop being shy and come inside."

The boy, who wasn't tall and must be Eren, entered the home. Like the doctor, he was fully cloaked by a raincoat, and his straight, black hair (just like the doctor's) was cropped short. He had a scarf wound around his neck. There was a hard, unpleasant look in his eyes. Mikasa realized she had seen that same look long ago on a wild dog that she and Father had come across in the forest. She decided she didn't want to have anything to do with the boy.

Eren, rudely scrutinizing the house's interior, finally rested his

eyes on Mikasa.

"Hello," Mikasa said timidly.

"Hello," Eren replied with a haughty snort. Mikasa had never heard such an unfriendly greeting. The stray dog had had perhaps a little more charm.

"Eren," the doctor warned with a heavy sigh before completing the introduction, which was that Eren was the doctor's only son and nine years old, like Mikasa. He had only one friend, so the doctor would appreciate it if Mikasa could get along with him.

At the mention that he only had one friend, Eren tried to object, but preempting him, the doctor said he would begin Mrs. Ackerman's exam and told his boy to go play with Mikasa.

Mikasa heaved a heavy sigh in her heart. Her rainy day was completely ruined.

"So I hear your mother is going to have a baby soon," Eren said as if he had suddenly remembered. The two were in Mikasa's room playing with dolls. Eren was fiddling with the "little brother" doll that Mikasa's mother had made. Maybe he'd grown bored with doll play.

Mikasa stopped changing the "big sister" doll's clothes.

"That's right," she replied proudly. "My mother says it's probably a boy. She said it felt completely different when I was in her stomach. She knows stuff like that."

"Huh…" Eren said, not sounding particularly interested. "But if it really is a boy I hope he becomes a great soldier."

Mikasa didn't exactly know what a soldier was, but she

imagined that it was someone who fought the beings called "Titans" outside of the wall. If that were so, she did not want her brother to become a soldier at all.

"Eren, are you going to become a soldier?" she asked.

"Yeah, I'm going to join the Survey Corps," Eren announced as if it were already decided. "I'm going to join the Survey Corps and go to the Outside World."

"The Outside World?"

"The world outside the wall."

"But aren't there Titans outside the wall?"

"You bet. We're going to butcher those brutes and—" Eren broke off as if he had said too much. "Hey, listen, Mikasa, right? You can't repeat what I just said to anyone—not about the Survey Corps or about the Outside World. You can't tell my father, or your parents, or anybody. If you say anything, I'm bonking you on the head."

With those words Eren made a fist and hovered it threateningly before Mikasa's eyes.

"I won't say anything."

"Are you sure? Do you promise?"

"I promise."

Eren stared intently into Mikasa's eyes as if to confirm that she wasn't lying. Under his gaze Mikasa felt like a small animal trapped under the hungry eyes of a wild dog.

"All right," Eren said, satisfied, before glancing out the window. The rain had stopped, but heavy rainclouds still hung low in the sky. Though Mikasa hadn't noticed it while it was raining, it

Lost in the Cruel World

looked as if the clouds were trying to hold the world down.

Eren flung the "little brother" doll onto the bed. "Let's go explore," he said.

Inside the forest it was dimmer, much colder, and as silent as a grave. Usually Mikasa would never go near the forest alone, for Father firmly forbade it. The forest was full of dangers, from hungry wild dogs to large boars with sharp tusks to many kinds of venomous snakes and insects, all of which carried an intense hatred for those who intruded upon their territory. However, far more dangerous than all of them was the possibility of getting lost deep in the heart of the woods. *Once you pass a certain point, you will never be able to find your way home.* Father had said this once. Once you got lost, the forest continued forever in every direction. Getting lost in the forest during the cold season, like now, meant freezing to death.

That was why when Father took Mikasa with him to the forest, he made sure they stayed near the edge, where it was safe. There Mikasa would pick nuts or watch young squirrels frolic; she would play in the small stream that flowed through the forest or even try to catch fish. So long as she stayed in that area, the forest was completely safe. It was trustworthy like her father, and kind like her mother.

But today, she had strayed far, far away from the safe place. The forest that they were walking through was different from the one that Mikasa knew. The tree trunks looked darker, a thick canopy of leaves hovered densely overhead, and the wind that occasionally blew through chilled the body to the bone. Mikasa couldn't hear the cheerful chirping of the birds, nor see any rabbit, squirrel, or other critter adorably scurrying about.

This isn't the same forest, she thought with a shudder.

Eren, however, seemed unconcerned and continued along a narrow path, hitting the tree trunks with a branch he'd picked up as he went.

"Hey," Mikasa said to his back as he walked a few feet in front of her. "We aren't supposed to go too far."

"Why?"

"Because my father said not to go too far into the forest."

"So?"

"So there are a lot of dangerous animals in the forest, and if we go too far we'll get lost and we'll never be able to find our way out."

"So?"

"So… So…" Mikasa couldn't think of any more reasons, so she stopped walking and said, "I'm going back."

Eren stopped in his tracks and looked over his shoulder at Mikasa.

"You're going back?"

"I'm going back."

Eren sighed heavily, as if annoyed.

"Hey, I said earlier that I was going to join the Survey Corps, right?"

"Yes."

"Your father goes hunting. Your mother gardens or cleans or does laundry or makes food. And she takes care of you. Your brother who isn't born yet will become a soldier. Right?"

"Yes," Mikasa agreed, nodding. She nodded, but didn't quite understand what Eren was trying to say. And the last part about her brother was something Eren had decided on his own.

The boy pointed his branch at Mikasa's face. "So then, what are you going to do?"

"…Me?"

"Yes, you. What are *you* going to do?" Eren shook his branch questioningly in a way that made Mikasa feel terribly uneasy.

"I'm…" Mikasa searched for an answer, but of course didn't know what to say.

What am I going to do in the future? She had never thought about such a thing. *I wonder what I'm going to do in the future… I'm going to live here with Mother and Father and my soon to be born little brother. I'm going to tend to the garden and take care of the chickens.* That was all Mikasa could think of, so that's what she told Eren.

"So," he said, poking her in the middle of her chest with the tip of the branch, "having no idea what to do, you're going to obey your father and never know anything but your house and the edge of this forest for as long as you live. You're never going to find out what lies in this forest. Is that right?"

Mikasa took the end of the branch between her fingers to soften the pain.

"Is that a bad thing?"

"It's not bad. It's not that it's bad, but you…you're no different from a chicken."

LOST GIRLS

"No different from a chicken," Mikasa repeated, without fully understanding.

"That's right. You own chickens, right? You're the same as those chickens. You have no idea what's going to happen to you, and you don't know what exists outside your fence. You'll go on thinking the tiny yard you live in is the entire world. Never doubting it, you'll get fed, you'll sleep, you'll get fed again, and then one day, suddenly, you'll get eaten. You're the same as those chickens."

Eren seemed to grow angry as he spoke. Or perhaps, from the moment Mikasa had met Eren—when they were introduced, when they were playing with dolls, when he was talking about the Outside World, while they were walking through the forest—he had been angry. At what? That was something only Eren knew. Or perhaps he himself didn't know. Either way, as his words piled up, his anger grew stronger and stronger, just like the vegetables in the garden grew larger.

"Like those chickens, you're gonna go on living without knowing anything, and you're gonna get killed without knowing anything," Eren said.

Killed? Mikasa thought. *By what? By a Titan? Maybe by the dangerous animals that live in this forest? Or maybe...*

"If you go home now, you'll never know what exists inside this forest," Eren went on. "You'll get killed without ever knowing anything outside your house and the edge of this little forest. That makes you the same as your chickens. Is that all right with you? Don't you want to know what lies in this forest? Are you all right with being a chicken? Well?"

26

Lost in the Cruel World

"I don't know," Mikasa said. She didn't know. *Why is this boy saying such things? Why does he keep calling me a chicken? Does he hate me for some reason? Does he say these kinds of things to other kids? If so, it's no wonder he only has one friend. Why did Dr. Yeager even bring him in the first place? And on a special rainy day. A day I was hoping to spend with Mother and Father.* As she thought all this, Mikasa grew sadder and sadder, and suddenly burst into sobs. "I don't know!" she repeated over and over again, her voice unstrung.

Eren seemed a little unnerved by Mikasa's sobs. He fretted, unsure of what to do, but eventually reached into his pocket and pulled out a crumpled, soiled-looking handkerchief. He handed it to Mikasa. Thanking him, she accepted it and wiped her tears. Then she folded it neatly and handed it back to him. Eren brusquely stuffed the handkerchief back into his pocket. He appeared to be lost in thought for a few moments, but finally spoke.

"There's nothing in this forest."

"There's nothing?"

"Yeah, nothing," Eren said, pointing his branch down the trail. It continued straight for a while and then curved to the right, out of view. "If you keep on walking down this path, you'll exit the forest. Once you exit, there are fields, and mountains, and villages, and then a wall. That's all. I saw it—long ago when I went to the interior with my father, I crossed this forest. It's much smaller than you think, and that's why I'm not afraid of it. I'm gonna keep on exploring. What about you?"

It was odd. After hearing Eren's words, Mikasa felt that the forest

LOST GIRLS

had lost some of its mystery. Of course, it was just as cold and gloomy as it had been before, and there was still no sign of the chirping birds or little critters, but Mikasa was no longer afraid. There was no reason to be afraid. The trees were just trees everywhere she looked, and the dense leaves that hung overhead were only leaves. *This forest is much smaller than I thought.* It was as if Eren's words had chased away something sinister that had been haunting the forest.

"I'm sorry," Eren said abruptly to Mikasa, who was walking beside him. They'd been continuing on the path for some time. "I didn't mean to say those things."

"It's fine."

"I'm just…sick of it. I'm sick of adults telling me to 'do this, do that,' or 'don't do this, don't do that,' and just calmly obeying them—I'm fed up with it." As he said this, Eren seemed to grow angry again, though his anger was more subdued than before. His body swathed in anger, he seemed almost like a severely injured animal caught in a net.

"It's fine," Mikasa repeated. As she did, she decided to become his second friend. It meant, at the same time, that she had made her very first friend. *Friends,* she thought. *I guess we're friends. If we're friends, I guess I could teach him some things. Like what kind of nuts to pick, or how to catch fish, or where to find the secret trail.*

Suddenly, from somewhere deep in the forest, the sharp, abrupt bark of a wild dog interrupted Mikasa's thoughts. It was a kind of bark she had never heard before. It wasn't the mad howl of a hungry beast, nor a threatening growl against an opponent in a

Lost in the Cruel World

fight, but rather cruel, as though it could become as coldhearted as it wished to be. Mikasa and Eren held their breaths, petrified where they stood. The silence continued to reign over the forest after that single interruption. Cold sweat ran under Mikasa's armpits. Her heart was hammering, and she felt short of breath. It was as if the air was thinning around her. Mikasa felt as if she had to run away immediately, but couldn't take a single step. It wasn't that she was paralyzed with fright—instead, something was urging her towards where the sound had come from. *You must go there, you must see what is happening there*, that something told her.

Caught in between, Mikasa could neither advance nor retreat. She found herself unable to take a step either way. Then, as if he could read her mind, Eren spoke.

"Let's check it out."

He took her hand. She gripped it tightly in turn. Mikasa felt as if she couldn't be scared with Eren. Together, they turned towards the sound and left the path for the wild, overgrown depths of the forest.

There's nothing in this forest, Eren had said earlier. *If you keep on walking down this path, you'll exit the forest. That's all.*

But, Mikasa thought, *what happens if you leave the path?*

They came to a field in a clearing. Ankle-high grass covered the ground, and a gray oval of sky stretched over their heads. For whatever reason, there was a space here, and smoke was still rising from a campfire that people who passed through the woods (though there couldn't be that many) used.

A pack of dogs stood as if to surround what was left of the fire, all of them gray and medium-sized. The pack was split into three groups of five or six dogs that each huddled together as if discussing some important matter. Of course, they weren't discussing anything—they were eating something they had caught. At a steady rhythm they buried their noses into their prey, tore the flesh, and chewed hungrily. A pair of legs jutted out of one of the circles, twitching and shaking. The animals were eating a human.

Mikasa stared wordlessly. She couldn't look away or close her eyes. She felt a strange numbness in her head and couldn't think about anything. The only thing she could do was watch the scene unfolding before her, her eyes agape and her mouth shut. She tried to squeeze Eren's hand, which she had already been gripping, to find that it was no longer there.

Weird—no sooner than Mikasa thought so, one of the cluster of dogs suddenly broke apart. It was the one closest to her. The dogs sprang away from their prey and let out low growls. Then, as if to follow suit, the remaining two groups of dogs pulled their faces away from their food to stare dully at Eren. He had thrown a stone.

The dogs rested their cold, empty eyes on him. Their noses were all wet with blood, and some had slimy pieces of meat stuck to their muzzles. They snarled with their snouts wrinkled, their sharp fangs on display, and drool swaying from their mouths. But they didn't attack right away. They knew they didn't have any reason to feel threatened.

Eren slowly pulled Mikasa's arm to tuck her behind him,

his hand trembling ever so slightly. As if to kill the trembling he grasped his branch with both his hands, but it looked all too pitiful as a weapon against more than a dozen feral canines. For what seemed like a long time to Mikasa (it may have only been a few seconds), Eren and the dogs stared one another down, neither party making a move. Then, a cool breeze blew between them. The trees rustled and dead leaves danced in the air. The dog closest to the children pricked its ears in response and lifted its face diagonally up, away from Eren. It looked as if it were at once thinking about something and about nothing at all. Or perhaps it was eyeing something that Mikasa and Eren couldn't see, listening to a voice that neither of them could hear.

As if giving up, the dog turned around and barked shortly at the others. Leaving both their half-eaten and untouched prey, they loped back into the depths of the forest.

Eren took a deep breath and let it out slowly. Three corpses were left behind, all of them brutally devoured. The throats were missing altogether; they must have been targeted first. The bodies had been pulled apart and their entrails dragged over the ground. The upper arms and thighs were covered in bite marks, and pieces of white bone shone through. The faces, however, were left unharmed, and revealed the corpses to be those of men.

One was middle-aged and bearded around his mouth and chin and wore a black knitted cap. Another was a little younger, with a mustache under his nose and a shaved head. The last, the youngest, had no defining features. The man with the hat held a knife, and the bald man a hatchet. They probably hadn't gotten the

Lost in the Cruel World

chance to use their weapons.

Mikasa's gaze swallowed the scene intently. It was the most gruesome sight she had ever seen, yet for some reason what had happened to the men seemed almost natural. *They got their just deserts,* she thought, though she didn't know why.

"What is going to kill me?" Mikasa asked Eren, who was beside her, her eyes still on the corpses.

"Kill you?" Eren asked back, sounding a bit surprised.

"You said earlier that I was going to get killed…that without ever knowing anything, I would get killed. What's going to kill me?"

"A huge force," Eren replied after a little while, as if he'd finally remembered telling her that. Then he turned his gaze back to the corpses of the three men. "You're going to be killed by a huge force."

"A huge force," Mikasa repeated. "Are you talking about the Titans?"

Instead of answering her question, Eren took her hand.

"Let's go back," he said.

The two children returned home and told Mikasa's father what they'd seen. They said they encountered the bodies while they were walking in the woods, and left out the part about almost being attacked by wild dogs. When Father brought back two military policemen from the village at the base of the mountain, Mikasa and Eren took them back to the place where the bodies lay.

That evening during dinner, Mikasa's mother and father spoke about the dead men and how they were people called "slave traders." That was what the military police had said. Mikasa wasn't quite sure what kind of people "slave traders" were, but from the way that Father spoke about them, she couldn't imagine that they were good people.

"But I wonder what such bad people were doing in a place like this." As Father said this, the color in his face drained as if he had just realized something. He looked at Mother. She seemed to have realized the same thing. With a pale face she returned her spoon to her soup and softly placed her hands on her stomach. Her hands were shaking.

"What's wrong, Mother? Are you okay?" Mikasa asked, worried. But Mother wouldn't respond, nor would Father. With their mouths closed, they didn't speak a single word until dinner was over. Mikasa didn't know what they had thought of, but it seemed like something that shouldn't be touched.

That night, Mikasa slept better than she ever had before. She didn't have any dreams.

❖

Eren started to accompany his father for the exams the doctor came to give every ten days. On those days, Eren and Mikasa would pick tree nuts, or watch young bunnies play, or catch bugs near the entrance of the forest, where it was safe. When the waning cold season came to a close, and warm, easy spring breezes took the place of the piercing winter winds, they played in the stream, or caught fish, or washed fresh vegetables from the garden and ate them. They sometimes walked aimlessly around the house feeding the chickens, which Eren had said would get eaten someday.

"This one lays eggs, so it's not going to get eaten," Mikasa explained to Eren, who seemed to understand.

The two no longer ventured into the deep part of the forest, and on at least one in three visits, they played with dolls in Mikasa's room. Eren may have been bored with it, but he always played without complaining. For lunch, they sometimes ate with Mikasa's mother and father and Dr. Yeager around the dining table, but the two usually sat outside in the warm sunshine and ate Mikasa's father's picnic meals. Then, after lunch, Mikasa and Eren said their goodbyes and parted ways, to meet again in ten days' time. Little by little, Eren grew used to Mikasa, and Mikasa grew used to Eren.

The anger that had been consuming Eren upon their first meeting now seemed to have retreated deep inside of him, and he no longer said upsetting things like "You're no different from a chicken" or "You're gonna get killed." Instead he spoke about life in Shiganshina District where he lived, and about his mother, and about his close friend Armin.

"Armin is really smart," Eren said. "He knows all kinds of things because he reads a lot of books."

"All kinds of things? Like what?"

"Like what? Well…all kinds."

"Does he know how children are made?"

It was a question Mikasa had been meaning to ask Dr. Yeager for a long time but always forgot.

"Wait, you don't even know that? Even I know," Eren said, appalled. "A big bird brings the baby in the middle of the night and puts it in the mother's stomach."

"How does the bird carry the baby?"

"It must put it on its back."

"It would fall off."

Eren thought for a moment. "Okay, then the baby is wrapped in a blanket, and the bird carries the blanket in its beak."

"That way it won't fall?"

"That way it won't fall."

Mikasa was persuaded. She tried imagining a big bird bringing a baby wrapped in a blanket. It was a rather lovely scene.

"But how does the bird put the baby in the mother's stomach?"

"Well, since it needs to go in, I guess through the mouth?" Eren said. "But anyways, Armin knows a whole lot about a bunch of things. He was the one who first told me about the Outside World." Eren went on to say that someday he would go to the Outside World with Armin. Eren told her that it was his dream. When he spoke about such things, he seemed truly pleased and particularly happy. Mikasa would go on listening to Eren, asking questions whenever she didn't understand something.

It must be a sign that he really sees me as a friend, Mikasa thought whenever Eren began speaking about such things.

Mikasa's parents and Eren's father, meanwhile, saw the children's relationship as being closer to siblinghood than friendship. But Mikasa, who didn't have an older brother, nor a friend before Eren, didn't know the difference between a friend and a sibling.

Lost in the Cruel World

Which of the two he actually was didn't concern her. To her, Eren was Eren, and that was enough.

Mikasa was fond of Eren, and Eren took good care of Mikasa. On days when the doctor visited, wherever they went, whatever they did, they were together. Mikasa now looked forward to Dr. Yeager's visits more than anything else in the world, even more than rainy days. Her only complaint was that she only got to see Eren once every ten days. The nine days that followed after every goodbye were so long, they seemed like an eternity. She wished that she could see Eren more often, and because she didn't know whom to ask, she wished on everything in sight: upon the stars in the night sky, the moon, the clouds, the vegetables in the garden, the chickens and frogs, the spiders that spun their nests below the eaves, and the darkness that greeted her when she closed her eyes in bed. Her wish was quickly answered when Mother caught a fever. For three days she was bedridden with a high temperature, and even after it abated, Dr. Yeager visited every five days to make sure her condition didn't worsen.

Mikasa was glad that her waiting periods had been cut in half, but at the same time she felt guilty that perhaps her wishing such a thing had made Mother fall ill.

After the fever, Mother began spending most of her time in bed. And when he wasn't out hunting or tending to the garden or cooking meals, Father spent every second at her bedside. Together, Mikasa and her father started taking on the tasks that Mother used to do. Mikasa got up early to water the garden, harvest the vegetables, and take care of the chickens. She also washed dishes, cleaned, and did laundry. And every day at noon, she made lunch and brought it to her mother's bedside.

As the days went on, their family conversed less and less. Before, Mikasa and her parents would talk about all kinds of things around the dining room table, over dinner and over tea after dinner, but that had become a thing of the distant past.

Seeing Eren was now Mikasa's only source of joy. In the afternoon after each of Eren's visits, and all through the following day, all Mikasa thought about was what she'd discussed with Eren and what she'd done with Eren. And on the couple of days before Eren arrived, all she thought about was what she would do with Eren when she saw him next. The days *in between* the visits hung in space, like a lonely little cloud floating in the middle of a bright blue sky, belonging to nothing, with nowhere to go. It seemed those days could disappear suddenly with the slightest breeze.

Like that, two seasons passed.

It was on a truly beautiful day, when a warm breeze was blowing from the south, that Eren arrived with wounds on his face. There were dark bruises below his left eye and at the corner of his mouth, and a raw cut split his lip. A large bandage covered his right cheek.

Stunned, Mikasa asked what had happened to him, but Eren said nothing.

"He got in a fight with some neighborhood kids," Dr. Yeager told her in his son's stead.

Eren still wouldn't speak about it. "Let's go," he simply said, and left the house.

Lost in the Cruel World

"In the Outside World, there's this thing called the Sea, and it's made entirely of salt water," Eren said, squinting in the soft light that bled through the trees. The children were sunbathing by the stream that ran through the forest, and Eren had spoken for the first time that day since his curt "Let's go," and for the first time ever about what the Outside World was like. Until then, he had only spoken relentlessly about how he wanted to go there to explore it, but never about the world itself.

In any case, Mikasa was relieved that Eren was finally opening his mouth. On the way to the stream, he had walked silently through the forest that had become his backyard, not responding to anything Mikasa said as she walked a bit behind him. It was as if the Eren she had first met had returned. Yet she wasn't uncomfortable as she had been during that initial walk through the forest; she felt that Eren could do as he pleased, and besides, it was a beautiful day for a walk.

After a while of continuing mutely through the forest, Eren had finally sat down on the bank of the stream, where for some time he just stared at the water rushing in front of him, occasionally throwing small stones into the current. And then, squinting in the soft sunlight that bled through the canopy, he began to talk about the Outside World.

"In the Outside World, there's this thing called the Sea, and it's made entirely of salt water." Eren continued, "And salt is like a pile of treasure, right? You'd think merchants would have harvested all of it, right?"

"Right," Mikasa agreed.

"But no. The Sea is so big it can't be harvested. The Sea is probably bigger than we can imagine. And the Sea isn't the only thing that the Outside World has. It also has 'firewater,' an 'earth of ice,' a 'snowfield of sand,' and other things. A world like that exists outside of the wall, and it's many times bigger than inside the wall. Isn't that amazing?"

"Yeah," Mikasa said, though in truth she didn't quite understand what was so "amazing" about it. Let alone the Outside World, she didn't know about anything outside of the mountain where she was born and raised. Mikasa had never once descended it, hadn't even been to the village at the foot. She had never even seen the wall that supposedly surrounded her entire world. To Mikasa, her house, her garden, the forest, and the fragmentary scenes from Shiganshina District described by Eren were the entire world. It was as if everywhere else was the Outside World.

"And Eren, you're going to go to that Outside World," Mikasa said.

"That's right."

"With Armin."

"Yes. I'm joining the Survey Corps with Armin and exploring the Outside World."

"When are you going to go?"

"It's still a long way off," Eren said, tossing stones into the stream while he calculated something. "When I'm twelve, I'll become a soldier in training, and then I'll train for three years...so in five years."

Lost in the Cruel World

"Six years," Mikasa corrected.

"Anyways," Eren said, tossing another stone into the stream, "about that long."

"You're going to wait six years?" Mikasa asked. Wait six years—Mikasa found it odd because she believed that Eren was the embodiment of curiosity. Maybe it wasn't the best way to put it, but it was almost as if he was *possessed* by his curiosity, his spirit of inquiry. Mikasa didn't know how he had come to be this way. Regardless, when he decided that he wanted to do something (or know something), no matter how dangerous, he immediately took action with no reservations and no room for compromise. Mikasa had witnessed it many times. Once, he'd reached his hand into a gaping hole in the ground, only to get bitten by a snake (that luckily wasn't poisonous). It had been a snake's burrow. If there was a hole—no matter how dark or deep, no matter what dangerous creatures might be lurking—Eren couldn't help but peer in or reach inside to see what it was hiding. That was Eren. That was why Mikasa found it odd that Eren would wait six years to go to the Outside World that he so badly wanted to see.

Mikasa asked once again. "Why are you going to wait six years?"

"Well, why don't you try casually hopping the wall without any training or equipment. You'll be in a Titan's stomach in an instant," Eren chided. "Besides, there are all these annoying regulations—it's not like you can just go outside the wall. It's not like leaving the house for a little bit of shopping. The only ones who can go outside the wall are members of the Survey Corps. Only the

Lost in the Cruel World

Survey Corps, unafraid of the Titans, goes to the Outside World."

"Why?" asked Mikasa.

"Why?" parroted Eren, looking at her as if she were the dumbest creature. "What do you mean, why?"

"Why are you going to the Outside World?"

"Forget why or how, I just want to know. The Sea, firewater, the earth of ice, a snowfield of sand—I only know those things by their names. I don't know what they actually are. I just want to know: what colors and shapes they have, how they smell. I want to know *what really exists in the Outside World*. But those guys—"

Eren stopped there abruptly. He made a fist with his right hand and punched his left palm repeatedly. Over and over again, as if he were trying to crush something imaginary. The sounds of his blows blended with the murmur of the stream as he punched, again and again.

"They're cowards," Eren muttered, after he stopped hitting his hand. Unfurling his fist, he stared at his open palms.

"They?" Mikasa asked, but her question didn't seem to reach Eren's ears.

"They're all cowards," he repeated. "They think everything is fine because it's peaceful inside the wall. They think the Titans could never break down the wall and come inside. They think, 'Why would you want to go to the dangerous world outside the wall? What are you gonna do if it leads the Titans in?' Armin said humans are meant to go to the Outside World, and he was called a 'heretic' and got beat up. That's the kind of world this is. They're all just hopeless cowards too used to being *domesticated*. And they all team up to keep us shut up inside the wall. They're…" Eren went on and on. Mikasa felt that as he spoke, the anger that had been nesting deep inside of him was crawling forth, slowly, like a snail inching across the ground, but steadily. It seemed that he was speaking in order to hasten its progress, but to where it was headed was a mystery. Perhaps it was to the Outside World, though for some reason Mikasa didn't believe that.

Either way, Mikasa didn't want Eren to return to Shiganshina District in his current state. She feared that if he did, he might get hurt even worse. In a couple dozen minutes, however, Dr. Yeager's exam would be over, and Eren would go back to Shiganshina. Nobody could stop it, and probably nobody could stop him from getting hurt. In that case, Mikasa at least wanted to be with him.

At some point, Eren's tirade had ended. His mouth closed, he was glaring at the small stream before him—or perhaps, at an imaginary point somewhere between him and the stream.

"Eren?" Mikasa called.

"I'm gonna join the Survey Corps and go to the Outside World," he answered, as though to convince himself.

He was going to join the Survey Corps and go to the Outside World. Mikasa would come to understand what that truly meant—whether she liked it or not—two days later.

It was one of those *in between* days. Mikasa ended up going alone to Shiganshina District, where Eren lived, on a day in between that floated in the bright blue sky like a lonely little cloud with nowhere to go. She went to deliver the hat that Dr. Yeager had

Lost in the Cruel World

forgotten during his visit two days earlier, which was when Eren had arrived with bruises on his face.

"I sent Dr. Yeager a letter to let him know that you're coming," Father said the day before Mikasa left. "You can just come back with him on his next visit, so don't worry about home for a little while and just have fun over there."

At nine years old, Mikasa didn't understand that her father was being kind. Aside from the half-days that she spent with Eren, she had often worked from morning to night since her mother had taken to bed with a fever. Mikasa was being allowed a few days of freedom. The decision owed in part, naturally, to the sheer generosity—Dr. Yeager would be lost without the hat that he always wore—of simple folk who lived surrounded by woods.

In any case, Mikasa was boarding a boat by herself to go to Shiganshina District on an *in between* day. For her, of course, both the boat ride and the trip to Shiganshina were new experiences. She did feel anxious about trying to go there alone, but more than that, she was overcome with joy at this surprise gift from her father, at getting to hang out with Eren during her gloomy *in between* days.

That morning, Mikasa awoke earlier than usual, finished her morning chores, and went down with her father into the village (it was a small village) at the foot of the mountain. She carried a cloth bag that contained Dr. Yeager's hat and the changes of clothes, lunch, and flask full of cold tea that Father had prepared for her. It was a windless, blisteringly hot day, and by the time they reached the village her entire body was drenched in sweat. She was the only one getting on the boat at the village, and only a few other passengers were aboard.

"Off I go," Mikasa said.

"Have fun," her father told her, patting her head.

After the boat departed, Mikasa explored the deck (it was a small vessel so it didn't take very long), watched the pastoral scenery drift by (the farm fields were several dozen times larger than her family's), and drank her cold tea and ate her lunch (a lettuce, tomato, and omelet sandwich and Mikasa's favorite, sweet, sweet, raisin bread!) on a bench. She tore a piece of her bread and tossed it to a cute little bird with blue flecks in its yellow feathers that was hopping across the deck. The bird took the bread in its tiny beak and flew off somewhere. When Mikasa finished her lunch, she was already in Shiganshina District. It had only taken a while, literally. How strange to think that Eren lived in such a nearby place.

He was waiting for her at the piers. Though it had only been two days since Mikasa had last seen him, when she set eyes on his bruised face, she felt as if she hadn't seen him in ages. For whatever reason, she felt a little nervous.

"Hey," Eren said, dripping with sweat. "You're lucky."

"Why am I lucky?"

"You'll see soon."

They were on their way from the piers to Eren's house when the loud sound of a bell cut through the air. Mikasa had been walking side by side with Eren down a road, staring wide-eyed at every sight that passed them by. She couldn't believe that the huge town

Lost in the Cruel World

was part of the same world as the mountain where she lived. She felt as if Shiganshina were the Outside World. Crowds of people and horse carts were coming and going, and buildings towered over her in lines—the town was overflowing with so many things. It was full of colors Mikasa had never seen, sounds she had never heard, and odors she had never smelled, and everything was combined, mixed together, intertwined. It was as if the town was one giant, living, creature.

And then there was the wall. Overwhelmingly intimidating, so tall it looked like you could touch the sun if you climbed it, the wall surrounded the town as if to keep the giant, living creature from escaping. Beyond that wall, Mikasa thought, was the Outside World where Eren so badly wanted to go. But it was also a dangerous world where Titans ate people. Imagining them made Mikasa a little nervous, but she felt secure looking at the wall.

Not even the Titans could break that wall down. That wall is protecting all of us—it was while Mikasa was thinking such things that the ringing of the bell pierced through the air. It was the loudest sound she had heard in her entire life. She clasped both her hands to her ears instinctively. The clanging made her feel anxious, as if it were a bell announcing a messenger bearing ominous tidings.

While the bell was ringing, everything in the town stood still, as if for a brief moment, the giant, living creature were ruled by the sound. And when the bell stopped, the creature suddenly resumed its movements.

"The Survey Corps is back! Let's go, it's a Heroes' Parade!" said Eren. He grabbed Mikasa's hand and started running.

LOST GIRLS

"Where did they come back from?" Mikasa asked while she ran.

"From beyond the wall, of course! This morning they went on an outside expedition. I told you you were lucky, didn't I? It's a lucky thing, being able to see the Survey Corps!"

The streets were already so full that it was almost impossible to wade through the crowd.

"Damn, I can't see," Eren cursed while he looked around restlessly. Eventually he found a wooden crate in front of somebody's home and climbed onto it. When Mikasa followed suit and stood beside him, they were just barely able to see beyond the throng. The spectacle that greeted Mikasa, however, was not at all like a Heroes' Parade, and she heard Eren gasp beside her.

The procession of the so-called Survey Corps as it returned from the Outside World to *this side* was relentlessly heavy and somber. The soldiers that made up the group looked uniformly injured, weary, and exhausted. Nearly all of them had bandages seeping with blood closer to black than red in color somewhere on their bodies. One soldier with only one arm was held up by his comrades, while another riding in the back of a cart was missing both his legs. The many layers of bandages wrapped around the stubs were soaked black. The troops continued through the crowd mutely as if they were criminals being led to prison. Not a single soldier looked forward, and every downturned face seemed completely expressionless. It was impossible to identify any kind of emotion. Anger, fear, hatred, sorrow, disillusionment, despair—all feelings had completely fallen away. What their eyes had seen in

Lost in the Cruel World

the Outside World was beyond Mikasa's imagination. *This is what a soldier is,* Mikasa thought. *This is the Survey Corps. This is what it really means to go to the Outside World.* Whether she liked it or not, she couldn't but see it now. *And,* Mikasa thought, *Eren is going to become a soldier, join the Survey Corps, and go to the Outside World.*

Mikasa shuddered and looked at Eren, who was standing beside her. He watched without blinking as the soldiers passed in silence. It was impossible to discern what he was thinking from his eyes, but in a diametrically opposite way from the inscrutability of the soldiers' state of mind. In Eren's eyes there was everything—anger, fear, hatred, sorrow, frustration, hope, disillusionment, despair—all mixed together. His eyes were watching the soldiers, but at the same time it seemed they were looking at something else.

It's hopeless, Mikasa thought. *You can't stop Eren.* The moment she thought this, everything went black. It was as if somebody had suddenly plunged her into a deep darkness.

In the darkness she couldn't see, or hear, anything. She couldn't even breathe. She tried to send some fresh air into her lungs, but they were plugged with the thick blackness with no room left for anything else. Mikasa clutched at her chest, to no avail, as the blackness flowed endlessly into her body. What pulled her out into the light was a woman's high-pitched voice.

"Moses! Moses!" an elderly woman emerged from the crowd screaming. She wandered into the procession and clung to a middle-aged soldier. "Um, my son Moses, I don't see him. Where is he?"

The middle-aged soldier turned to a young soldier beside him and instructed, "It's Moses' mother. Bring *it* over."

The elderly woman looked up at the middle-aged soldier as if she were looking at a strange animal she'd never seen before. The younger soldier brought back a cloth bundle from somewhere and handed it to the middle-aged soldier, who handed it over to the elderly woman. She looked at the bundle, then gazed at his face again, puzzled. The soldier didn't say a word.

The elderly woman timidly opened the bundle, let out a brief shriek, and quickly closed it. Before she could, Mikasa caught a glimpse of what was inside from where she stood on the crate. It was only for a moment, but plenty of time for the image to get burned into her mind.

The thing in the bundle was the right arm of a person. It had been covered with wounds, and white bone peeked out from some of the gashes. The thumb, middle finger, and ring finger had been missing nails, exposing the naked flesh underneath. The entire limb had been a very strange color, like murky swamp water and chicken droppings mixed together. Mikasa could hardly believe that she'd witnessed a human limb. It had been more like some unfortunate, harmless fish that was loathed by people for its size and grotesque appearance.

"That was all we could take back," the middle-aged soldier stated in a pinched voice. The elderly woman clutched the bundle to her chest and crumpled to the ground. Her wailing was strange and like nothing Mikasa had ever heard. In response, the crowd began whispering amongst themselves: *how sad, how pitiful, how gruesome, can't be helped, they did go outside the wall, at least she got*

Lost in the Cruel World

an arm back, no, it would have been better to get nothing back. As if to cover up their words, the elderly woman wailed on and on even more loudly.

Mikasa didn't want to see or hear anything more. She wanted to grab Eren's hand and immediately get away from the place. The crate that they stood on, however, was so densely surrounded by people that she couldn't move an inch. She knelt down on the box and covered her ears with both her hands, but couldn't completely block out either the crowd's murmurs or the elderly woman's shrieking wails. Muffled, the sounds were somehow even eerier. She clutched the bag her father had packed for her that morning. It held Dr. Yeager's hat and a change of clothes, a flask, and a cloth that had wrapped the lunch that Father had prepared for her, peaceful artifacts from a peaceful world. The bag was the only thing that connected Mikasa to that peaceful world, and as if to cling to it, she held on with all her strength, just as the elderly woman cradled the bundle that contained her son's arm.

All the while Mikasa thought about one thing: *You can't stop Eren. Nobody can stop Eren. Not Dr. Yeager, not Eren's mother, not Armin, not Mother or Father, and of course, not me.* Eren would eventually become a soldier, join the corps, and go to the Outside World. He would return injured, weary, and exhausted, his body covered in bandages soaked black with blood and missing an arm or a leg or an eye or an ear. No, there was no guarantee that he would return at all. Perhaps he would as just an arm wrapped in an ominous shroud. *And nobody can stop him. If that's the case,* Mikasa wished with all she had, *I hope this Survey Corps gets crushed.*

Somebody just smash the Survey Corps. She clutched her bag and fervently wished for this.

When it all finally ended, Mikasa lifted her face. Beside her, Eren watched in a daze as the Survey Corps disappeared from view. The streets were so deserted it was difficult to imagine they had been brimming with people just moments earlier. The Heroes' Parade was over, and the citizens must have gone back to whatever they needed to do. Only those who had no reason to hurry, perhaps, or nowhere to rush off to lingered in the street talking to one another. Before Eren and Mikasa stood one such pair, an older bald man and an unpleasantly overweight middle-aged man whose body swelled like a balloon.

"Damn tragedy," the fat man said, his gaze trailing the fading Survey Corps.

"We're basically fattening those brutes up with our own taxes," the bald man complained.

Mikasa felt Eren stiffen beside her. *I have to stop him,* she thought, but it was too late. He'd already punched the back of the older man's shiny bald head.

"What are you doing, you stupid brat? Come over here," Bald Head said, grabbing Eren by the collar and dragging him into a narrow alley between two houses.

Mikasa watched impassively as Eren disappeared into the alleyway. Bald Head and Fat Guy had taken him away so fast that she didn't even know what had happened.

"Ow! Brat bit me," Bald Head's voice came from inside the alley. It was followed by a sharp *whack!*

Lost in the Cruel World

Mikasa knew exactly what that sound was. Once, long ago—and she knew only of one time—Mother and Father had been having an argument. Mikasa didn't know over what, but Mother had said "Coward!" and slapped Father's face—*whack!* It was the same sound.

Hearing it brought Mikasa back to herself, and she ran for the alley.

"Listen, kid, don't you go underestimating adults," Bald Head said, striking Eren in the face. His small body flew and his back smacked against the wall.

"Now, now, leave it at that. Don't be fighting a brat," Fat Guy chided, snickering.

"Shut it, Piggy. This kid hit me out of nowhere," retorted Bald Head.

"It's because you were making fun of the Survey Corps!" With that shout, Eren sprang up to kick Bald Head in the groin, but just before the blow landed, he was grabbed around the ankle and treated to a head-butt. Blood started gushing from Eren's nose.

"Ugh, disgusting," Bald Head said, sending Eren flying across the alley with a kick of his own. "Did you see that, Piggy? The brat tried to kick my unborn sons. Earlier he bit me, and well, before that, he suddenly punched me in the head. I hadn't done a thing to him, and he started fighting me. Disciplining dangerous, filthy, stupid kids like him while they're still kids falls on us grown men, don't it?"

Fat Guy snickered some more. "When you put it like that, it sure sounds right and proper, you gotta discipline dangerous, filthy, stupid kids while they're still kids. He's just like a dog, you gotta discipline a dog."

"Don't we?" Bald Head said proudly, pulling Eren to him and hitting him once more. Thick blood ran from Eren's nose.

"It falls on us, it's an adult obligation to discipline dangerous, filthy, stupid kids, because dangerous, filthy, stupid kids like him become soldiers and gobble their free meals, and saunter outside to get eaten by Titans, and let the taxes that we poor workers pay with the sweat of our brows all go down the drain. What's more, they act superior towards us poor workers who're feeding them!" Bald Head kicked Eren in the stomach after saying this. The sound was horrible, and Eren shuddered as he gasped for air.

"Well, well, well, it's Eren, isn't it?"

Mikasa turned around to look behind her. Three not-so-bright-looking kids stood in the alleyway.

"Hey, you brats, this isn't a show. Get lost!" bellowed Bald Head.

"Um, help Eren," Mikasa begged the three boys. They didn't react at all to her words and instead started addressing Bald Head—*Easy, easy, easy, why so uptight, pops, we'll be a good audience. You know, pops, that idiot's name is Eren, he's a persistent bastard, that one, even though he's a weakling. We beat that idiot up, now when was that again, when was it that we beat up the stupid idiot? Dunno, two days before yesterday, maybe four days ago? Hey, "two days before yesterday" is like, you just mean three days ago, doesn't matter, anyway, pops, you know what, that kid is like those heretics, one of those crazy heretics with the stupid, idiotic, moronic idea that humans are meant*

Lost in the Cruel World

to eventually go to the Outside World, so discipline him a little, pops,
we'll cheer you on as hard as we can—

The word "heretic" seemed to add gunpowder to the flames of
Bald Head's rage.

"What, a heretic?!" he said, grabbing Eren's hair and slamming
his face into the ground. "So on top of being dangerous, filthy, and
stupid, kid, you're also with the heretics? Huh? Well? Say it. Say it,
say it, say it," Bald Head shoved Eren's face into the ground over
and over and over again.

"...kill you," Eren said, gasping. "I'm gonna kill you all. Gonna kill you. I'm not afraid of you. I'm not..."

Fweet fweet fweet! the boys whistled through their lips and
their fingers. *Go, Eren, go, Eren, go, beat up baldie—*

Bald Head let go of Eren's hair only to deliver another kick in
the abdomen with a broader arc than before. "Kill me? You gonna
kill me? Did a little kid just say that to a grown man?" He buried
his shoe in the same spot again, and the contents of Eren's stomach spilled out. "Hey, what do you think you're doing, soiling the
pavement maintained with the taxes we workers kill ourselves to
pay?" He kicked Eren again, and Eren vomited again. This time it
was liquid, with blood in it, and Eren folded over and retched out
every last drop of it.

Fweet fweet fweet, go go go, way to go, pops! Fweet fweet fweet.
A bottle suddenly flew down from the sky, hit the ground and
shattered, scattering countless shards of glass and a sour-smelling
brown liquid that burned the nostrils.

"What do you think you're doing?" A middle-aged woman

was leaning out of the second-story window of one of the houses. She was naked from the waist up, and her freckled breasts drooped unattractively as she shouted. "If you're gonna fight, do it somewhere else. It's so loud I can't sleep."

Fat Guy snickered and told her, "Sorry, ma'am, we're almost done. Right now we're in the middle of disciplining a dangerous, filthy, stupid kid."

Bald Head added, "Think of this as being for the good of the world, of the people, and of you too, lady. A little patience."

"Well now, that's a really sweet story, but couldn't you do it a tad more quietly? With all the retching and whistling, it's too noisy and I can't sleep. I was up humoring drunkards throughout the night and I'm tired, and from the morning I have to listen to all this retching and whistling? Give me a break."

Sorry! the young boys said in chorus.

"In any case, disciplining him or whatever it is you're doing, do it quickly and get out of here. Really, on a sunny day like this you should at least let me sleep in peace," the middle-aged woman grumbled and slammed the window shut.

During the exchange, Mikasa held Eren up and tried to help him escape from the nightmare.

Hey, pops pops pops, Eren's gonna escape, some weird girl is trying to escape with Eren, the boys said.

Bald Head stepped in front of Mikasa, blocking her way. "Hey, missie, that's not okay, tut! Where are you trying to take that brat?"

"Um, um, sorry," Mikasa stuttered through sobs. "Please let us go. Please."

Lost in the Cruel World

"No, no, no, we can't let this brat be." Bald Head grabbed Eren from Mikasa's arms and yanked him down to the ground. "He really is a dangerous, filthy, stupid kid and on top of that he's with the heretics. We need to discipline him properly because his sort ruin our world. Let this dangerous, filthy, stupid kid do as he pleases, and before long the world will be broken. Dangerous, filthy, stupid kids like him go on to wreck our peaceful world, and missie, wouldn't you be unhappy too if that happened? That's why we sensible adults have to discipline dangerous, filthy, stupid kids *juuuust* right. Yeah, kid? Am I wrong? Hmm, am I wrong?" Bald Head kneeled down and grabbed Eren's hair and shouted right into his ear, "Well? Answer me!"

Eren didn't say anything. Bald Head huffed and slammed Eren's face into the ground and kicked his stomach again. Eren coughed up blood.

Mikasa heard a clattering sound in her head—*klaklak*. Slowly she bent down and picked up a piece of the bottle that had fallen at her feet. Out of several she chose one that was larger and easy to hold, and that had a sharp, pointed tip. Even Mikasa didn't know what she was doing. She understood, though, that nobody was going to help Eren, in which case the only option was to protect him herself. She turned towards Bald Head and took a step.

"Now come, missie, over here. Just watch with uncle," Fat Guy said, clasping Mikasa firmly from behind. The shard that she'd been holding slipped out of her hand. Fat Guy was soaked with sweat, and his body reeked of rotten fish. Mikasa twisted her body to escape his embrace, but the man's grip was as solid as rock and didn't give an inch. He glued his lips to Mikasa's ear and spoke:

"That man over there is very good at teaching what's what. It's his specialty. He's taught dog, after dog, after dog just like that. So let's relax and leave it all to him. Your friend punched him in the head out of nowhere and even threatened to kill him—what a frightful thing for him to say. That's really, really dangerous and wrong, so he has to undergo his proper punishment and discipline. That's a child's duty."

Aww, I'm getting kind of bored. I'm getting bored too, shall we go? Yeah, but where? Like somewhere fun, that's where, the not-so-bright-looking boys said to one another and left the alley.

Meanwhile, Bald Head lifted Eren up by his hair. "Hey, kid, did you know? If I pull your hair hard like this, it's good for you—it'll make you smarter. My old man told me that. He was a dirty, stupid, good for nothing, crazy bastard like you, but he was right about that. If I pull your hair hard like this, it stimulates your brain, and you'll get smarter and smarter. My old man used to say that, and you want to get smarter too, don't you? If you get smarter you won't go punching people in the head out of the blue, you won't go saying disturbing things like 'I'm gonna kill you,' and you won't go hanging out with the heretics. It's not okay to go punching people out of the blue or to tell them disturbing things like you're gonna kill them, and it's not okay to hang out with the heretics. It's really not okay. You don't understand that one bit. It was just like my old man said. The number one thing that dangerous, filthy, stupid kids need is to be disciplined." As Bald Head

spoke, spit flying, he slapped Eren's cheek over and over and over again. Finally, he dug his knee into Eren's stomach, and then, as if satisfied, the man hacked up sticky pea-green phlegm from deep in the back of his throat and spat it at Eren. "I'm getting hungry," he noted, and with that, Bald Head and Fat Guy left the alley.

Mikasa didn't move a muscle, and for a little while she stayed still while the strong sunlight slowly baked her skin. The sour smell of the brown liquid from the shattered bottle and Fat Guy's rotten fish odor lingered in the alleyway.

❖

Mikasa sat in a chair by the bed as she watched Eren's back. He slept facing the wall. The setting sun's rays that streamed in through the curtains hanging from the window right above the bed made pools of orange light on Eren's body. Cool air floated in through the open window, as did the quiet sounds of the neighborhood's dusk hustle.

When Eren finally awoke, he asked Mikasa, "How long have I been asleep?"

"Not for long," replied Mikasa.

In the two days that followed, Eren hardly spoke. Except when he ate and went to the bathroom, he lay in bed and stared out the window. Mikasa gazed out too, as silent as Eren.

From his room on the second floor, Mikasa could see rooftops and, far beyond them, the towering wall. The smoke from

Lost in the Cruel World

the chimneys that jutted out of the roofs drifted in the wind, and occasionally a few birds flew over the wall to the Outside World. When Eren grew bored of looking out the window, he napped. Even then, Mikasa sat in a chair by his bed and spent the time watching his sleeping face or staring out the window. When she did sleep, it was still in the chair and leaning over on his bed. Eren's mother (Aunt Carla, that is) cautioned her that sleeping like that was bad for the body and made a bed for her in the next room. She also offered to take her son's friend, who had come all the way to town for a visit, on a little outing, but in each case, Mikasa thanked her and politely declined.

Fortunately, the injuries that Eren had suffered weren't life-threatening. His nose was broken, and his face was swollen, but his abdomen, despite being kicked repeatedly, was only bruised. Dr. Yeager said that his bones and his internal organs were unharmed. The bald-headed old man must not have had the strength to inflict any lethal damage even to a nine-year-old boy. Had that younger, larger man been the opponent, Eren might have been killed.

Still, Eren refused to tell Dr. Yeager and Aunt Carla how he'd gotten hurt. He said that he fell, and stuck with that story. Mikasa didn't say anything, either, under Eren's strict gag order.

Leaning on her shoulder as they stumbled home from the nightmare in the alleyway, he'd forbidden her from speaking to anyone about what had just happened. Not to Dr. Yeager, not Aunt Carla, not Mikasa's mother or father, nobody at all.

"Do you promise?"

LOST GIRLS

"I promise," Mikasa had said. She'd promised not to tell anybody about the Survey Corps or the Outside World the first time they'd met, and felt almost nostalgic. And like that, Mikasa and Eren had carried their secret together and said nothing, spending two days staring out the window for long moments, sometimes sleeping, exchanging words now and then. On the morning of the third day, it was time for Mikasa to return with Dr. Yeager to the mountain where she had been born and raised.

She went to say goodbye to Eren when she had gotten ready to leave. He was asleep facing the wall once again, and for some reason, he looked so small. Watching his back, Mikasa felt her chest tighten. She wanted to hug him as hard as she could, but felt that it would be wrong, and didn't. *Goodbye,* she said in her heart and gently closed the door.

❖

"Is there any way you could bring yourself to tell me why Eren was put in that condition?" Dr. Yeager asked Mikasa, who was sitting beside him on a deck bench and watching the pastoral scenes drift by. The weather, somewhat cooler than it had been on the day Mikasa arrived in Shiganshina, was that much easier to bear. There were many passengers, and a few children around Mikasa's age were running around excitedly on deck. Mikasa shook her head.

"I see," Dr. Yeager said with a sigh. "The truth is, I put in a request for an investigation to the Garrison. I have an acquaintance over there, who'll handle it. Because Eren is the kind of boy that he is, there is no way he will share what happened, no matter who asks what, but of course I know that that kind of injury wasn't caused by any fall. So, Mikasa, you don't have to tell me *what happened*, but do you think you could bring yourself to tell me simply *who was there, and what that person looked like*? If you could tell me, it would be extremely important to the investigation. What do you think?"

Mikasa considered what to do, but eventually decided to say nothing. She had a feeling that once she opened her mouth, she wouldn't be able to stop herself from spilling everything, including Eren's desire to join the Survey Corps and go to the Outside World. The thought crossed her mind that if she confessed all that, perhaps the doctor would stop Eren, but she couldn't break her promise—either of them. She kept her mouth shut and shook her head even more resolutely.

Dr. Yeager sighed again. "I'm sorry, Mikasa. I won't ask you about anything anymore, so you don't have to worry." He seemed incredibly tired as he said this, and twice as old. It was the first time she'd seen such a look on the doctor, who was always so vibrant and kind and reliable. Mikasa wanted to say anything that might give him a little peace of mind but couldn't find the words.

"I have a feeling that Eren is walking towards a dangerous place without even knowing it himself," let drop Dr. Yeager, his eyes cast down at the deck floor. "Even Aunt Carla and I don't know what that boy is really thinking in his little head. All I know is that he always seems as if he is angry at something, and that his anger is sending him off to a dangerous place. I have no idea where the anger is directed, though, or why he has to be burdened with it. That's why I started taking Eren to the mountain where you live. I thought that, perhaps, getting away from town for brief spells and experiencing nature with you might bring about a good change in him."

Mikasa nodded like a doll.

"Listen, Mikasa, I just can't understand why Eren had to be so severely beaten. I have no guess as to why anybody would do such a horrible thing to a nine year old, no matter how hard I think. Even if Eren had done something wrong, there should be absolutely no need for someone to hurt him physically to such an extent. But the reality is that someone did."

There the doctor paused. As if just remembering, he took off his glasses, pulled a neatly folded handkerchief out of his pocket, wiped his lenses, and put them back on. The joyful shouts of the children running about the deck floated softly on the wind.

"This world looks peaceful. There's a tall, sturdy wall and the Titans can't come inside—for now, at least. Either way, we've made ourselves a provisionally peaceful world. In terms of the Titans, this is true. This world, however, contains a variety of menace and evil wholly different from the Titans. That is what I believe. It's not something that can be seen, but it takes various forms and, one day, suddenly shows itself to us. It can afflict anyone. You could say we are surrounded by this thing. And perhaps this time it ensnared Eren, in the form that it did."

A few of the children cheered as they ran past Mikasa and the doctor. He watched them scurry about the deck for a little while before continuing.

"However, Mikasa, I'm also thinking, perhaps this was something beckoned by Eren himself. Something in Eren as a person fatally attracts it, the menace and evil—"

"A huge force," the words abruptly left Mikasa's lips. She, herself, didn't know why she'd uttered them.

A huge force—those were the words Eren had spoken deep in the forest the first time they'd met. He'd done so looking upon three corpses that had been devoured by wild dogs. Mikasa would be killed by a huge force.

"A huge force," Dr. Yeager repeated, pondering the words' meaning. "A huge force, hm? Perhaps that is what it is. Maybe we are all surrounded by a huge force that our eyes cannot see. And perhaps it is this huge force that so angers Eren." Having muttered that much, Dr. Yeager caught himself and quietly shook his head. "Well, I'm sorry, Mikasa. What am I saying? Why am I discussing this with you?" he admonished himself, laughing. When the doctor laughed, deep wrinkles gathered in the corners of his mouth.

More than half of what the doctor had said was too difficult for Mikasa, but she felt like she understood the gist of it.

"Perhaps only you can protect Eren from this huge force," the doctor reprised as the village at the foot of the mountain came into view.

Mikasa looked up at his face in surprise. "Me?"

"That's right. I have a feeling that the only one who can protect Eren is you," the doctor said. "In any case, I think he'll be able to come along for the next checkup. It would make me very happy if you continued to be his dear friend."

"Yes," answered Mikasa.

Eren, however, didn't come along on the doctor's next visit. Nor on the one after that, nor on the subsequent occasion.

"Eren's injuries haven't healed?" Mikasa asked Dr. Yeager.

"Oh, right, he still isn't feeling well, it seems," he replied. It wasn't difficult, however, to guess that Dr. Yeager was hiding something that he couldn't bring himself to tell her.

Based on their conversation on the boat, the doctor certainly wanted to bring Eren. Eren, however, was refusing. Why? Of course, nobody answered Mikasa's question. Or rather, nobody knew the answer. Nobody besides Eren.

Mikasa wrote Eren a letter:

> *Dear Eren,*
> *Hello. How are you? Are your injuries better?*
> *This morning we picked tomatoes and cucumbers from the garden. We ate them for breakfast. They were very delicious tomatoes and cucumbers.*
> *The chickens are happy too. This morning there was an egg.*
> *A lot of nuts have fallen in the forest.*
> *I want to pick nuts with you again.*
> *I hope you will get better soon. Please write back.*

It was that sort of letter. After thinking for a little while, she added

Lost in the Cruel World

the words "I miss you" at the end. Then she put it in an envelope, sealed it firmly, and gave it to Dr. Yeager.

No response came from Eren.

Mikasa stopped asking Dr. Yeager about Eren. She felt as if there was no point and didn't want to trouble the doctor any further.

After Eren stopped coming, Mikasa felt like she'd been robbed of something in her. It was a kind of thing that she could never regain. She seemed to recall that some such thing had happened to her somewhere before, but she couldn't remember when or where. Either way, that part of her was left as a blank space that nothing whatsoever could fill. Every sight she saw was faded in color, every sound was muffled, and everything she ate was flavorless.

Mikasa started working far harder than she ever had. She woke up early in the morning to draw water from the well, to water the garden, and to harvest vegetables. She fed the chickens and collected any eggs. Then she went to the well to draw water again, and cleaned, did laundry, and washed the dishes. Along with breakfast, she made the packed meal that Father took hunting, and she cooked lunch for Mother and herself and dinner for the three of them.

For nine-year-old Mikasa this was heavy labor, and for the first few days her body screamed, but before long she grew used to it. As long as she was working, Mikasa at least didn't have to think about the blank space that she couldn't handle that had appeared in her all of a sudden.

Whenever she had the time, she went into the forest alone

and walked the path she'd walked with Eren. A lot of things had changed since he'd stopped coming, but the forest was still the same old forest. The thick trees, and the nuts that fell along the path, and the murmuring stream, and the wild rabbits that scurried about, and the families of squirrels that chewed peacefully on nuts—all of those things reminded Mikasa of Eren.

In such a way Mikasa spent her days. When the doctor was scheduled to visit, she awoke earlier than usual, completed her chores more quickly than usual, and waited for Eren to arrive. But always, the only person who came climbing up the mountain path was Dr. Yeager. Each time Mikasa confirmed this, she sighed inwardly and spent the next five days in the same way. It was like the *in between* days stretched on and on. Those days *in between*, with no destination, would continue for eternity. Mikasa thought that maybe she wasn't ever going anywhere again.

Her five days recurred, over and over. The hot season ended, and the cool, refreshing one went as well, no sooner than it had arrived. Chilling winds signaled the coming of the long, harsh cold season. It even snowed a couple times. Mikasa turned ten. And on the night she turned ten, she arrived at a conclusion.

Eren wasn't coming back no matter how much she waited. He wasn't coming back, probably ever. Yet there was nothing Mikasa could do. All she could do was wish, just as before, when she'd wished upon anything in sight. She wished on even more things now, and more earnestly, to *please let me see Eren.*

It was soon after that Mother's condition, even as the baby was almost due, deteriorated.

LOST GIRLS

"She's showing symptoms of preeclampsia," Dr. Yeager said during his visit, sounding awfully sorry.

Then, after a lengthy conversation between the doctor and Mother and Father, it was decided that Mikasa's family would move close to Eren's home in Shiganshina. Though moving Mother so close to childbirth posed a significant risk, if she were in Shiganshina, Dr. Yeager could attend to her right away if something were to happen. So that was that.

That night Father killed and roasted a chicken for dinner—probably because there was no way to bring them to Shiganshina, and also because he wanted to treat Mother to a nutritious meal. Mikasa couldn't bring herself to lay a hand on the chicken dish, though.

After dinner, Father remained at the dining table alone, drinking and smoking, which was rare for him. He swallowed the liquor in his small glass in swift gulps and breathed out heavy sighs along with the wafts of tobacco smoke.

Mikasa watched this version of her father, from behind him through a crack in the door, but quietly shut it before long and went to her mother.

She was sitting up in her bed knitting, and Mikasa crawled in beside her.

"Oh my, oh my, what a little baby you're being," Mother teased, but moved aside to make room. Mikasa pressed her ear to Mother's swollen belly. She heard soft sounds—*tump, tump*—which somehow made her feel sad.

"Mother, I'm sorry," Mikasa said, not knowing herself why she

Lost in the Cruel World

was apologizing. Tears spilling over her cheeks, she buried her face into her mother's chest and cried. "I'm sorry."

Mother started to say something, but in the end remained silent and gently pet Mikasa's hair. As she did so, Mikasa soon fell into a deep sleep.

❖

Mikasa's new house was close to Eren's—just two minutes away if she ran. The moment they were done moving, she headed over to his place. However (as she half expected), he wasn't there.

Aunt Carla came to the door and said, "Sorry, Eren's not home right now." When Mikasa asked if she could wait until he was back, Carla welcomed her in with an "Of course," showed her to a chair, and brought out some black tea and a fruitcake.

"Where is Eren?" inquired Mikasa as she stuffed herself with the fruitcake. It was far sweeter than her favorite raisin bread.

"He's out playing with Armin," Carla, seated across from Mikasa, answered after sipping some of the black tea. "It's been like this for a while. He leaves in the morning and returns in the evening. That's been Eren's daily routine, from shortly after you visited Shiganshina, I think. I have no idea what they're doing or where they go. But today, I told him that you were moving here, so he might come home earlier than usual."

That was when Dr. Yeager returned. He wore his usual hat, carried his usual bag, and wore his usual coat.

"Ah, Mikasa, there's something I want you to take a look at. I just went to your house, but heard that you had come here." As the doctor said this, he exchanged a glance with Aunt Carla.

She stood up and said, "I'm going to do some shopping. Mikasa, you make yourself at home," then left, gently closing the front door behind her.

"What I want you to look at is this."

Settling in the chair where Carla had sat, Dr. Yeager pulled two pieces of paper, each folded in four, out of the pocket of his overcoat, and spread and placed them on top of the desk. On the two sheets were portraits. One depicted Bald Head, who'd roughed up Eren, and the other was a sketch of Fat Guy, who'd spoken to Mikasa with his mouth glued to her ear.

"Are these the two men who hurt Eren?" the doctor asked.

Mikasa clamped her mouth shut.

"You don't have to speak," assured Dr. Yeager. "Eren told you not to say anything, didn't he? So either nod, or shake your head. That way you won't be breaking your promise. Right?"

"Maybe," Mikasa said after thinking for a moment. Indeed, Eren had only told her not to *speak* about it to anyone. Just moving her neck might not count. Maybe.

"Are these the two men who hurt Eren?" the doctor repeated his question.

Mikasa still wasn't sure, but in the end she nodded.

The doctor glanced at the two portraits and sighed. "I'm sorry I made you remember something horrible. I asked Eren the same thing, but that boy wouldn't give me an answer. So I had to ask you. I won't tell him that you told me." Dr. Yeager folded up the sheets and returned them to his pocket as if he couldn't stand their sight a moment longer. Then he seemed to hesitate a little, but spoke again. "Those two men are dead."

"Were they killed?" Mikasa asked reflexively.

"Killed?" the doctor echoed. He seemed a little surprised. "Why would you think that?"

Mikasa didn't know why, either.

"They died in an accident, the day before yesterday," the doctor said. "Some people from the Garrison who were conducting an investigation determined that those two were probably the ones who hurt Eren. A few passersby had seen them pull Eren into an alleyway. When Garrison personnel spotted them walking in the street and tried to talk to them, the pair started running. They entered a narrow alleyway, dashed through it, and bolted out to a thoroughfare, where a wagon carrying a lot of heavy cargo was rattling along. The fat man was run over, and the other man was kicked by a horse and then flattened by the cargo."

The doctor paused there. Mikasa silently waited for the doctor to continue.

"According to an eyewitness, Eren had attacked the bald man out of the blue. Even so, those men shouldn't have gone that far. It was hardly just or fair. They received their just deserts," the doctor concluded, speaking more to himself than to Mikasa. "They invited their own deaths," he appended, like some postscript to a finished letter.

Then, saying that he needed to report her confirmation to his Garrison acquaintance, Dr. Yeager left the house. With his permission, Mikasa waited for her friend in his own room.

It hadn't changed at all from when Mikasa last visited. She placed a chair by his bed and sat down, just as before. The sun shining in through the window made pools of light on the perfectly made, empty bed, and outside she could see the rooftops and chimneys of neighboring houses and the wall. Smoke rose up from the chimneys and drifted in the wind. It was a quiet afternoon, with only Eren missing from the picture.

Mikasa touched a part of the bed that was in the shade. None of Eren's warmth remained, and she felt only the coolness of the sheets. Mikasa bent over on the bed and closed her eyes like before, trying to remember Eren. The only image that floated to her mind was the faces of the two men. Bald Head and Fat Guy. Mikasa tried imagining their deaths. Fat Guy had been run over by a wagon. Bald Head had been kicked by a horse and flattened under heavy cargo. They had received their just deserts, according to the doctor.

They got their just deserts, Mikasa thought. She knew those words. On the day she'd first met Eren, she'd thought them looking upon the corpses of the three men devoured by wild dogs in the depths of the forest: *They got their just deserts.* But even now, she didn't know why she'd thought such a thing.

They invited their own deaths, the doctor had also said. Perhaps it was true. Perhaps it wasn't. Perhaps they (those five men) had been killed by the *huge force.* The idea crept into her consciousness alongside the cool air of a still afternoon.

Lost in the Cruel World

Perhaps she had fallen asleep. Somebody shook her body, and when she opened her eyes, Eren was there. He sat on the edge of the bed watching her. Mikasa raised herself and stared back at him intently for a little while. Then, as if to make sure that it really was him, she touched his fully healed face.

"Hey, lay off," Eren said, fleeing her hand.

It was definitely the real Eren.

"Were you asleep?" he asked.

"I don't know," she said.

The two of them left the house and went for a walk along the riverbank. The sun was still high, but an evening mood was already setting in. The town had slipped out of the quiet afternoon and seemed to be regaining its liveliness.

Just like when they'd first met, Mikasa was trekking a few feet behind Eren. She'd been meaning to talk about all kinds of things, but now as she walked with him, she couldn't find the words. She didn't mind, however. He seemed much happier than the last time she'd seen him, and after not seeing him for so long, it was more than enough that she was getting to walk with him again.

At the same time, they couldn't go on like that forever. There was one question that Mikasa had to ask. Not asking it meant never moving forwards, or backwards.

"Hey, Eren, why didn't you ever visit again?" she went ahead and tossed the question at his back. It came out in a voice that was so small it surprised her, and she wondered if perhaps it didn't reach him.

"I'm sorry," Eren said after a little while, and then sank into silence once more. Maybe he was considering whether or not to answer her question, or how to answer it. Or maybe he'd decided not to.

Somewhere, somebody was playing an instrument and singing a song. Along with a raspy male voice, the pleasant notes of a stringed instrument rode the soft breeze to Mikasa's ears. As she walked behind Eren, who was still silent, she opened her ears to the song, which blended with the shouts from the street shops.

> Two children walk hand in hand
> They go walking over a bloodstained road
> The two of them whisper to each other, some secret talk
> They're planning on how to change the world
> If you're alone, then you're alone
> I wish I could do something too
> I sometimes wonder if there isn't something I could do
> With somebody else, in harmony

Eren seemed to have spoken.

"What was that?" Mikasa asked him.

"I said the Survey Corps is gone," Eren told her. "Because they couldn't come up with any results no matter how many outside expeditions they conducted, they got squashed."

Mikasa couldn't say anything. She just waited for Eren to continue.

"The gate was even plastered shut. Now nobody can leave,"

Lost in the Cruel World

Eren went on. "I told you before, didn't I? That all these cowards were teaming up to try to keep us trapped inside the wall."

Mikasa nodded her head. The Survey Corps was gone. Eren's dream had been crushed by people whose faces he didn't even know. His chance of going to the dangerous Outside World had been completely ruined, but deep down, Mikasa was relieved. She felt bad towards him for feeling that way but nevertheless thought, *Now Eren's life won't be in danger.*

She quickened her pace and caught up to him.

"Hey, Eren."

"That's why Armin and I have decided to go to the Outside World on an Airplane."

"The Outside World, on an Airplane?" echoed Mikasa, not understanding a bit of it. The Outside World on an Airplane—what on earth could that mean?

"Right now, Armin and I are building an Airplane. I was so busy with that that I couldn't go to your place. I'm sorry," Eren said. "An Airplane is a machine that flies in the air like a bird. But it's dozens of times bigger than a bird. Armin and I are gonna ride the thing, get over the wall, and go to the Outside World."

Eren explained that Armin's parents had tried to go to the Outside World on an Airplane two years earlier but had failed, and died. The Airplane's wreckage had been found along with both of their remains on this side of the wall. The details were unknown, but the Military Police Brigade had ruled it as an accident. Armin's parents had hidden the plans of their machine in a secret location,

LOST GIRLS

and Eren and Armin were trying to improve upon them. From as early as he could remember, Armin had watched from the sidelines as his parents made the Airplane, and since he'd turned six he had even started helping them, so he knew the basics. Furthermore, Armin had determined the reason for his parents' failure and come up with a solution.

That was about the extent of what Eren said, but most of his words didn't reach Mikasa's ears. As he spoke, she remembered what Dr. Yeager had said to her that day on the boat: *Eren is walking towards a dangerous place without even knowing it himself. His anger towards a huge force that our eyes cannot see is sending him off to a dangerous place.*

Flying an Airplane to the Outside World was exactly that. *And,* Mikasa thought, *the huge force that killed those five men (maybe) is now trying to ensnare Eren.*

Perhaps only you can protect Eren from this huge force, Dr. Yeager had also said.

But that was a mistake. Dr. Yeager was wrong. *I can't protect Eren. He hasn't given up going to the Outside World, even though the Survey Corps is gone. And somehow he has come up with this thing called an Airplane. Even if the Airplane is completely destroyed, Eren will find another way of going to the Outside World. I can't protect him. Nobody can protect him. In the end, only Eren can protect himself. But he'll never want that because he can only protect himself by abandoning his desire to go to the Outside World.*

"Mikasa, you were right," Eren said. "You asked me why I was gonna wait six years to go to the Outside World. You were right.

78

Lost in the Cruel World

You were exactly right. It would be stupid to wait six years. The Airplane is almost finished, and once it's finished, I'm going to ride that thing and go to the Outside—"

As if something had just occurred to him, he suddenly broke off there and stopped in his tracks to look at Mikasa, who had stopped as well.

"When is the Airplane going to be finished?" Mikasa asked.

"It won't even take ten days."

"...Oh."

"Hey, Mikasa, about this—you can't..."

"Tell anyone," Mikasa finished. "I promise."

"Yeah." Eren then closed his mouth and didn't speak again for half a minute. "I'm just so fed up."

"Uh huh."

"With all kinds of things, I'm so fed up."

"I know."

❖

For the next ten days, Mikasa fell into a strange calm. It was as if something inside of her had died when she parted with Eren. That something became a cold, hard lump that fit perfectly into the blank space that had appeared after Eren stopped coming to the mountain, and it was never to be dislodged. Carrying the thing in her, Mikasa sank into a vast feeling of helplessness and spent her days as if she were gazing at fading lights. She tried going to Eren's house a number of times, but he was never home. Each time, Aunt

LOST GIRLS

Carla or Dr. Yeager looked at her apologetically. Seeing their faces hurt her, so she eventually stopped going. Eren was trying to go to the Outside World on an Airplane with Armin. She thought perhaps she should tell his parents, but felt that even if she did, it would be of no use. In the end she didn't say anything.

During those ten days, a severe chill came down from the north, and the coldness that enveloped the world was too harsh for it even to snow.

That afternoon, Eren came to Mikasa's house and gave her a butterfly. It was in a wooden box with netting on the sides that was filled with various plants and flowers. Perched on a blade of grass, the butterfly was completely still. It was so white as to be almost transparent, so white that its wings almost let you see through to the other side.

When Mikasa gently shook the box, the butterfly fluttered around as if it had no choice, but soon alighted on a blade of grass again and grew still.

"It's yours," offered Eren. "Rare, right, a butterfly in winter? Armin made that container."

"Thank you," Mikasa said.

Eren paused a moment before opening his mouth again. "The Airplane is finished."

"When are you leaving?"

"Tonight."

"Really."

"Yeah, tonight."

Lost in the Cruel World

"Can I ask you one thing?"

"Sure."

"Don't die."

"Hey…" Eren said, appalled. Then he tried to smile, perhaps to comfort Mikasa, but couldn't pull it off.

"Don't die," Mikasa repeated.

"We'll see each other again," assured Eren. "The Airplane only carries two passengers, so we can't do it this time, but once we land in the Outside World and get settled, I'll come back alone. Then I can take you there, too."

A cold wind blew between them. Mikasa clutched the box that held the butterfly as if it would help her stay warm. Watching her, Eren seemed to hesitate for a moment, but eventually took the scarf around his neck and tossed it over her shoulders.

"I'm only letting you borrow it," Eren warned. "It's warm, right?"

"It's warm."

"You keep it safe until I get back, okay?"

Mikasa gave a straight nod and stared at Eren's face. She began to say something, but stopped.

"What is it?"

"Take care," Mikasa said.

"You too," Eren said.

Gazing at his receding figure, she thought to herself: *This is probably the last time I'm going to see Eren.* Even if Eren made it safely over the wall to the Outside World, Mikasa would probably never see him again. Perhaps that was something that couldn't be helped.

When he turned a corner and she couldn't see him anymore, Mikasa turned back into her home and placed the wooden box with the butterfly on the desk in her room. The setting sun was shining through the window, and there wasn't a sound to be heard in the hushed, empty house. With her due date so close now, Mikasa's mother had begun staying at Dr. Yeager's. Father was at her side and wouldn't be back until nighttime. Mikasa sat for a while and stared at the butterfly, which remained still inside the box, but soon grew bored and went for a walk.

It was a long walk. She ambled down an avenue, cut through an alley, continued along the riverbank, crossed a bridge, then proceeded along the wall.

A festival was being held in town that day, and the sounds of flutes and drums floated through the air. The gate leading out of the wall (the Titans' only point of entry) had been plastered shut, and the townspeople were celebrating eternal peace. More people than usual filled the streets, all of them dressed up and chattering to one another as they headed in roughly the same direction. Mikasa gave the scene hardly any thought.

As she walked, she thought about Eren. She thought about the days they'd spent together and the conversations they'd had. She thought about the rainy day when she'd first met Eren, about walking through the forest with him, about picking nuts, about watching squirrels and wild rabbits frolic, about playing in the stream and catching fish—about those quiet, peaceful, gentle days.

No matter what Mikasa did, however, she couldn't remember

Eren's face. It was an image that should have been within arm's reach, but when she reached for it, it quickly disappeared. The only thing she could remember was his back. She remembered it from when she followed him in the forest on the day they met, and from when he led her through the streets of Shiganshina. It was the back as she walked a few feet behind him, the back as he slept facing the wall in his room, and the back that had receded only moments ago. *We only just saw each other and said goodbye,* Mikasa thought. *Eren is leaving tonight, and from now on I'm going to have to spend my days without him, and I can't even remember his face. I'm going to go my whole life without even being able to remember his face, and one day...*

You're going to be killed, Eren had said.

Right, she was getting killed. By a huge force.

I'm going to go my whole life without being able to remember Eren's face, and one day I'm going to be killed.

Devoured by wild dogs in the forest, run over by a wagon, kicked by a horse, crushed by heavy cargo, or perhaps, beaten by two nameless men in a dingy, sour-smelling alley, Mikasa would be killed. Or—

On a rainy day, someone knocks on the door. *Knock knock.* The sound is ominous.

"Pardon the intrusion," the men say as they enter. Their faces are familiar. The three of them were killed and devoured by wild dogs in the forest.

The first man stabs Father and kills him.

Lost in the Cruel World

The second man uses a hatchet to kill Mother and the baby in her womb.

Then the third man strangles me to death.

Just like that, one day, the huge force captures me all of a sudden. I die helplessly, without being able to remember Eren's face.

No way. That is just wrong. It simply mustn't happen.

I'm going to see Eren again, and I'm going to get a good look at his face. I'm going to carve his face into my heart and never forget it. I still have some time left. It might not be very much time, but still, there is some time left. I'm going to go see Eren.

When Mikasa made up her mind, she was in a plaza. She wasn't sure how she'd gotten there, but she imagined she'd been taken up by the flow of dressed-up people who filled the streets. In any case, she was in a plaza.

At its center was a group of performers plying their trade: a strongman breaking chains with his muscles, a magician swallowing a long sword up to its hilt, a puppeteer pulling the strings on two soldiers and a Titan, a man skewering his own body with long and thick needles, a woman beating a drum as she sang eerie songs, and dwarves dancing around to her music. A rope was put up around the performers, and the people gathered around it whistled, clapped, shouted, and sometimes threw copper coins into the roped-in area. The slanting sunlight dyed everything orange.

What is this place? Why am I in such a place? When did I find my way here? Many questions arose in Mikasa's mind, but they didn't matter: *I'm going to go see Eren.*

LOSC GIRLS

She tried to walk towards the exit, but couldn't move. People were packed in all around her, and all of them were trying to go their own way. To begin with, she had no clue where the exits were, nor could she stand still long enough to search for one. Whenever she tried, she was shoved by the rushing crowds and almost fell over. Not only did the plaza reek of sweat and alcohol and tobacco and other unknown odors, but the cacophony of whistles and laughs and screams and vomiting and strange melodies and drumming also blended together and assaulted Mikasa from every direction, and she began to feel sick.

"Um, please let me through," she said, but nobody seemed to have heard her. All the people around Mikasa were talking, drinking, laughing with their mouths wide open, kissing each other, cursing at each other.

What are these people doing here? Mikasa wondered. *They can't even see the street performers because it's so crowded.*

Somebody bumped into the man who was drinking right behind Mikasa, and she felt a cold dribble on her head. "Hey, what do you think you're doing? You made me spill my booze!" the man complained, to which the other person said, "It's your fault for drinking out here," and a fight began.

As the man raised his fist, his elbow struck Mikasa's face, and she fell to the ground. Blood dripped from her nose. Whether it was alcohol, or water, or sweat, or urine, the ground was very damp. She crawled on it to try to get away, but—*Hey hey, idiots, don't be starting a fight now!*—was surrounded by the feet of several people who came to break things up. Mikasa was stomped on her hands, on her legs, on her back. A clump of her hair got stuck to a clasp on someone's boot and tore from her head with an awful sound. Another shoe's pointed end jabbed her in her side. Mikasa coughed violently and curled up to protect herself. *Why is everyone getting in my way?* she thought. *All I want is to see Eren.*

"Stop, stop, stop, you're ruining the festival!" somebody cried, while someone else shouted, "Go, go, go! This is way better than the performances." A third yelled, "Yikes! You're in the way," and kicked Mikasa away.

With that, she was finally able to crawl out of the center of the whirlpool. She stood and wiped the blood from her nose. Then, weaving between the crowds as they surged forward, she tried to find an exit. That was when somebody suddenly grabbed her arm.

The man who had grabbed it pulled her into the roped area and up onto a low shabby stage made of wooden crates.

Mikasa was totally lost.

"Ladies and gentlemen!" the grabber of her arm said in a terribly cheerful voice. It was grating, like metal scraping. "Behold as I, hypnotist extraordinaire, turn this pure and innocent little girl into a murderer through my marvelous mesmerism! A rare sight indeed! Ladies and gentlemen, feast your eyes!"

Everybody nearby was watching the fight, though, and no one looked over. Seemingly unfazed by this, the man continued to speak.

"Ladies and gentlemen, you doubt me. But of course, but of course, if I were you, I would be doubtful as well. To think that such a cute and innocent little girl would become a murderer is unimaginable! Yet I can do this. Nothing is impossible for your hypnotist extraordinaire, the renowned Mirror Man! Now, young miss, look at my face."

The man wore a raven-black cape, and underneath, a bright white shirt and a red necktie. His pants and his tall boots were jet-black like his cape. On his face he wore a mask with a mirror stuck to it.

"Um, please let me go," Mikasa said and tried to shake herself free, but the Mirror Man's grip on her arm was as solid as stone.

The Mirror Man crouched down and stared into her face. The mirror pasted onto his mask was curved to fit his visage, so the reflection of Mikasa's own was distorted.

"If I let your hand go, where do you plan on going, young miss?" the Mirror Man asked. It was as if her own reflection in the mirror was speaking.

"I'm going to go see a friend," Mikasa said.

"Going to go see a friend," the Mirror Man parroted. "Well, this isn't good! Your friend must be waiting. You can't keep your friend waiting. You should hurry along."

"Thank you," Mikasa said, relieved, but the Mirror Man maintained a firm grip on her arm.

"Yet I cannot simply say 'yes, of course' and let you go, young miss." The Mirror Man tightened his grip on Mikasa's thin arm. "I have work to do, you see. I have to make you a murderer with my mesmerism. That is my job. It's a worthless job, but if I don't do it, I can't feed myself. What a predicament we have. The young miss wants to go see her friend, and I don't want to let her go. Such a

Lost in the Cruel World

predicament. What are we to do?"

"I don't know," Mikasa said. *How would I?*

"You don't know. You don't know, huh. Then how about this?" The Mirror Man gleefully held up a finger. "How about you kill me right now. That would make my performance a success, and you'll be able to go to your friend right away. Both of our goals will be achieved at the same time. I can, of course, hypnotize you to make you kill me, young miss, but that will take some time, and that is not something you desire. So, young miss, kill me right now."

"Kill you?" Mikasa asked. "Me, kill you?"

"That's right," the Mirror Man said. "Naturally, you must not want to do any such thing, young miss. You must feel that this is extremely absurd. But that cannot be helped. This world is built on such things. This world is built upon the absurd. Isn't that true? Humans don't want to be eaten by the Titans, and yet, the Titans ruthlessly devour humans. Isn't that true? It is something that cannot be helped. It is something about which we have no choice. Now, young miss, kill me."

The Mirror Man said this and opened his cape wide. Several knives hung in a row inside. He grabbed one of the knives and made Mikasa hold it. It was a short but sharp knife.

"Um, somebody..." Mikasa tried to ask for help, but all of the people around her had their backs turned watching the fight. The men who'd come to break it up had been sucked into what was now a pandemonium.

"To tell the truth, I'm fed up, myself," the Mirror Man

whispered in Mikasa's ear. "I'm going to have to stage my hypnotism for this audience all night. My job is to spend all night staging my hypnotism in this loud plaza that smells as it does. Tomorrow, when this is over, I will go to a different town, to a different festival, and stage my hypnotism there. That's my job. Standing atop this shabby crate in this idiotic costume, I stage my idiotic hypnotism before an idiotic audience. And when it's over, I go to yet another town, to yet another festival. That is my life. That is how I have lived up until now, and that is the only way I can go on living. It is a meaningless and barren life. You agree, don't you, young miss? Don't you think that it is a meaningless and barren life? But that is something that cannot be helped. It is something about which I have no choice. Until I die, all I can do is go on living this life. And from the bottom of my heart, I'm fed up with it. So tonight, in this noisy, smelly plaza, I have decided to stage the performance of my lifetime. It was when I saw you that I came up with the idea, young miss. A lantern turned on suddenly in my head. 'That's it, I'll stage the performance of my lifetime. I will use my mesmeric art to make this pure and innocent little girl kill me in front of a large crowd.' This will be my last hypnotism, and my revenge on this world."

Maybe this man is crazy, Mikasa thought. *I can't make any sense of a single thing he is saying.*

"Now, what will you do, young miss?" the Mirror Man asked. "You don't have much time. If you don't decide soon, you'll run out of time. Tick, tock, tick, tock, time is passing. It passes without pause. Nobody can stop it."

Lost in the Cruel World

It was just as he said. At some point the surroundings had grown darker, and the torches that had been lit were coloring the night sky. *If I don't hurry, Eren will leave. Why is everybody getting in my way?* thought Mikasa. *All these different people are teaming up to get in my way.* As she thought this, she felt for the first time that she understood how Eren felt.

"Tick, tock, tick, tock," the Mirror Man whispered again in Mikasa's ear, "you should hurry. Otherwise, you will never be able to see Eren again."

Mikasa looked at the Mirror Man's face. The only thing she saw, however, was her own distorted reflection. The face in the mirror wore a terribly astonished expression. Mikasa gathered her breath and timidly asked, "Sir, who are you? How do you know about Eren?"

"Sir is nobody," the Mirror Man spat. "But at the same time, he is everybody. I am a hypnotist extraordinaire, the renowned Mirror Man. I can become anybody, but at the same time, I can be nobody. And hypnotists know a lot about all kinds of things. Well, enough of that. What I'm trying to say, young miss, is that you are lost. You got lost and strayed here of your own accord. We'll say that's fine. You must have needed to. The problem, though, is that you've remained too long. It's time to go back where you belong. If you don't, you'll never go back again. In other words, without being able to remember Eren's face, you'll be shut in here for your entire life. You don't want that, do you?"

Mikasa didn't say anything. She just gripped the knife, stared at her distorted face reflected in the mirror, and listened to the

Mirror Man speak. The voice was the Mirror Man's, but it also sounded like it came from far away (from the depths of her own self, perhaps). It had sent her deep into the forest the day she'd first met Eren, the voice of that *something*.

The same voice said from within the Mirror Man's mask, "If you don't want that, kill me. If you want to get out of here, you have to kill me. If you want to return to where you came from, blood has to be spilled. Of course, if you wish, you may remain here for as long as you like. You can leave, you can stay. You can choose either. Now, what will you do?"

"I…"

"Yes, you. What are *you* going to do?" asked Eren.

What are you *going to do?* The first time Mikasa had met Eren, he had asked her that question in the forest. Pointing the tip of his branch in her face—*What are* you *going to do?*

However, the face of the Eren who said this was a blank space. Mikasa just couldn't remember his face. *What am I going to do?* she wondered. *What do I want to do?*

"What do you want to do?" It was again Eren who asked.

I want to see Eren. What I wish for, what I have been wishing for all along, is only that. I want to see Eren, if only for a few seconds. I want to see him just one more time. I want to get down from this shabby wooden crate, escape this filthy plaza, and go see Eren as soon as I can. But to do that I have to kill this crazy man who is standing before me. Kill? I could never…

"I could never…do that." Mikasa was shaking. Tears streamed down from her eyes. *Why is everybody getting in my way? All these*

people are teaming up to get in my way, and all I want to do is see Eren. If I could see him, just one glance would be enough for me. Am I not allowed even that?

No, the world would not allow even that.

If that's the case, Mikasa thought, *if that's the case then this world can get broken. I hope someone wrecks this world. Completely, ruthlessly, wreck it with no trace left behind.* As she did, she noticed a clattering sound—*klaklak*—in her head. She remembered hearing that *klaklak* back when (how long ago was it?) the bald man had beaten Eren up before her eyes.

Mikasa gripped the knife more tightly. *And if nobody can wreck this world,* she thought, *I will.*

At that moment, the night sky flashed bright for an instant. Before the afterimage of the burst of light could even disappear from the sky, there came a tremendous, thunderous roar that seemed to split the earth apart. Then the ground shook. Reflexively, Mikasa pointed her eyes up at the wall, though she didn't know why she chose to look there. She couldn't see anything above the wall, however—only the rainclouds that had taken over the sky.

After the roar of thunder, a thin rain began like an afterthought. The fight that had been in full swing broke up. The plaza became eerily silent, and all that could be heard was the *pitterpatter* of the fine rain.

Suddenly, a woman screamed. The screech sliced the damp air to pieces. Everybody turned to look at her. She was pointing her finger at something. Mikasa, too, looked to where the woman was pointing.

Lost in the Cruel World

A male corpse lay on the ground. It was the Mirror Man's body, dead there at Mikasa's feet. The knife was buried deep in his heart; his hands clasped its wooden handle. His cape was spread wide open and his bright white shirt was soaked red.

Mikasa's clothes were covered in blood spatters. Nobody said anything. Mikasa also didn't say anything. It was as if time had stopped.

In that world where time had stopped, the first thing to move was the Mirror Man.

"Now, ladies and gentlemen, were you able to witness it?" he said, rising up. He spoke in his original grating voice that sounded like scraping metal. "The hypnotist extraordinaire, the renowned Mirror Man, has amazingly turned this innocent girl into a murderer," he declared, beaming. Pulling the knife from his chest, he let out a merry *hahaha*. His jarring laughter blended with the quiet sound of rainfall and floated through the plaza.

"As you can see, the blade of this knife is designed to retract." As the Mirror Man pushed on the tip with his finger, the blade sank down into the handle. Then he held up his hands, smeared thickly with blood. "And this is chicken blood. I hid it on myself earlier." He let out another merry *hahaha*.

"However," he said, raising his finger, "however, the fact that this innocent girl stabbed me has not changed. That truth is immovable. Not even a Titan could move it. This young girl stabbed me in the heart with this knife. *Snick!* Just so. That fact, no matter what anyone says, cannot be changed. Ladies and gentlemen, what say you of the skill of the hypnotist extraordinaire, the renowned

Mirror Man?"

There was a sprinkling of half-hearted claps from the crowd. A few people threw copper coins at the Mirror Man's feet. "Thank you very much. Thank you very much." The Mirror Man bowed his head as he lovingly picked up each and every copper piece.

How stupid—it was just a trick—how boring—and on top of that it's started raining, the audience mumbled as they left. The Mirror Man was still on his hands and knees gathering his copper. Mikasa got down from the wooden crate and put the plaza behind her.

When she arrived at Eren's house, he had already left for the Outside World. But she knew he would be gone. When she'd seen him earlier that afternoon, she shouldn't have simply let him go. She should have stopped him then, by force if necessary. No matter what anyone said, no matter how much Eren fought back, even if it antagonized the entire world, she should not have simply seen him off. She should not have given up. Mikasa understood that perfectly.

A little while after Mikasa arrived at Eren's house, the baby was born safely.

Just as Mother had said, the baby was a boy. Mother, who had given birth, and Father, who had held her hand all through the birth, and Dr. Yeager and Aunt Carla, who had helped with the birth, were all completely exhausted.

Their faces couldn't look happier.

Lost in the Cruel World

The four of them were laughing joyfully. The baby was crying heartily. Mikasa carved their faces into her heart so she wouldn't forget them.

That will do, somebody said. *Time to go home.*

Maybe, Mikasa thought.

Before long, the front door opened, and a boy entered the home. He had sandy hair. He was drenched and mud-stained from head to toe. Mikasa knew the boy. She was meeting him for the first time, but she knew him well. It was Armin—Armin Arlert, Eren's childhood friend.

He was weeping. Mikasa knew what Armin was about to say. She hoped her prediction was wrong, but of course, it wouldn't be. Bad feelings always came true.

"The Airplane didn't fly," Armin finally said, kneeling on the floor. His voice was heavy with sobs. "It didn't even lift an inch off of the ground. It's all my fault. We were living in a dream. We were crazy with a fever. I should have known, but didn't think it through. There was no way a nine-year-old kid could make an Airplane. It's my fault that Eren... It's because I said, 'Let's build one.' It's because I told Eren about the Outside World. It's all my fault. The Airplane slid down the hill. We couldn't control it at all. Eren grabbed me and hurled me off. Then, with him still on it, the Airplane ran into the wall... I'm sorry, Mikasa... Eren took my place... I couldn't do anything... Sorry..."

Bad things always happen on rainy days, somebody whispered to Mikasa.

LOST GIRLS

❖

Inside the wooden box, the butterfly was as still as ever. Mikasa gazed at it for a while, but eventually opened the window and removed the net. The butterfly still didn't move. Mikasa shook the box. Sighingly, the butterfly took flight, and like someone who didn't know which way to go, fluttered about in front of Mikasa's face. Then, as if it had decided at last, it exited through the window.

Outside it was raining. It quietly refused to let up. The butterfly disappeared into the gentle rain.

Time to go home, somebody said again.

Right, Mikasa thought. *It's time to go home.*

3

When Mikasa opens her eyes, it is still raining. It is a fine rain, almost closer to fog, quiet, cold, and without personality.

The butterfly is still dancing before Mikasa's eyes. Adrift between a blood-soaked earth and a gray wet sky it flutters aimlessly, elegantly. Somewhere in the distance sound the Titans' footsteps, and the screaming, the groaning, the wailing. Mixed in with the scent of rain is the odor of freshly spilled blood.

Right, Mikasa thinks. *This is a battlefield.* Rain falls into her eyes. Her vision becomes blurry. She blinks, and her vision clears a little.

The butterfly is gone. It has disappeared in the split second that Mikasa had her eyes closed. Perhaps it finally found a place to go, or a place to return to. Then Mikasa notices that it has stopped raining as well. It ceased with the butterfly's departure.

She feels as if she has awoken from a very long dream. Yet she can't remember what it was about. Try as she might, she can recall nothing except for a sense that it was a happy, and sad, dream.

❖

LOST GIRLS

It is no dream, however. Nor is it an illusion, or a delusion. It isn't even a parallel world existing alongside the one that Mikasa lives in. What she has witnessed—"experienced" might be the more accurate term—is no dream, no illusion or delusion, nor a different world, but rather a nameless something. Perhaps her soul left her body and strayed into a nameless place that subsists in a separate time, a separate space. In any case, having slipped through that nameless something (or someplace), Mikasa finally understands. What that something or somewhere was, she will never know, but from the depths of her soul she gets it.

No matter how far she pulls Eren away from danger, death is going to capture him. It isn't that he is destined to die. Nor is it fate. Rather, it's due to *something* that Eren includes as a person. No matter the circumstances, that *something* guides him towards death, or conversely, draws it in. Yet nobody can rob him of that *something* because it is what makes Eren the person he is. Without that *something*, Eren would not be Eren.

Mikasa gets this. Or perhaps it needs to be rephrased thus: *The understanding could visit her only now that she has slipped through the yet unnamed place, and blood has been spilt there.* Either way, when Mikasa comes by this understanding, she accepts Eren's death as a stark fact. She has no choice but to.

❖

Again, Mikasa thinks. She lifts her heavy arm. Her hand grips a sword broken off at the hilt. *Again, this again. Again I lost my*

Lost in the Cruel World

family.

Mikasa arises and gets down from the roof. Her steps carry her. Her body is horribly heavy, and cold. The chill that seeped into her marrow has grown firm roots.

That's it, Mikasa thinks. *Enough.* She drops down to her knees, and sits down. *Do I have to remember this pain again, start from here again?*

The Titans' footsteps resound, and slowly approach her.

That's it. Enough. There's no need to start anything anymore. Mikasa returns the sword in her left hand to its sheath.

A Titan halts right by Mikasa.

This world is cruel. And so beautiful.

The Titan reaches for her.

It was a good life.

Mikasa closes her eyes. *That's it. Enough. Time to end this. There's no need to start anything anymore, no need to go anywhere.* She tries to bring the sword in her right hand to her neck.

Sooner than she is able to, the Titan closes its fist around Mikasa. Yet the hand grasps thin air. Mikasa has sliced off the Titan's fingers.

She slips past the hand that stretches for her a second time, and swings her sword again. She slips through the Titan's hand again and again.

What am I doing? thinks Mikasa in her clouded mind. The Titan launches her into the air, and she tumbles across the ground. She coughs, and gets up. Her body is as heavy as before.

Still she stands. *Something* stands Mikasa up. *Why get up? Why struggle? What for? There's no reason to live anymore.*

Behind Mikasa, another Titan appears. As if it has been roaming, wandering around the battlefield with nowhere to go and has just happened to stray into this place, the Titan appears.

The first Titan stands before Mikasa. Grinning broadly, it approaches her.

There should be no reason to go on living. Mikasa thinks this again. However, *something* urges her on. It is the *something* that stood her up. It is the *something* that made her swing her sword. It is probably the same *something* that Eren includes as a person. That *something* whispers to Mikasa's body. It whispers to her soul. *Fight,* it says.

"Fight," Eren says.

Fight? Mikasa thinks.

"That's right, fight! You have to fight!"

Fight. You have to fight.

That day—*that day* when the cold rain fell—while one of the vulgar men choked his neck, Eren had said, "It's win or die... If you win, you live... If you don't fight, you can't win."

If you don't fight, you can't win. If you win, you live.

I'm sorry. Mikasa's cheeks are streaked with tears. They keep flowing, on and on. She feels their warmth on her cheeks. It soaks deep into her marrows and starts to thaw the chill that has grown roots. *I'm sorry, Eren. I won't give up anymore. I'll never give up again. If I die, I won't even be able to remember you.* With both hands, she grips her sword, her tiny blade. *So no matter what, I must win.* She wills strength into her hands. *No matter what, I'll live!* She summons all the strength she has.

    "Ahhhhhhhhh!"

4

"AAAAAAAAH," the black-haired Titan lets out a war cry, erect by the steaming corpse of the fallen Titan. With all the strength in its body, at the top of its lungs, it screams its never-ending war cry.

Mikasa watches the spectacle before her in complete bewilderment, and at the same time, with slight euphoria—because it almost seems to embody humanity's sheer fury.

While Mikasa is immersed in her bewilderment and slight euphoria, something in the depths of her soul, outside her consciousness, makes a wish on the black-haired Titan exulting before her. Just as she did sometime, somewhere, to the moon and the stars in the night sky, to the vegetables in the garden, to the chickens and frogs, to the spider that spun its web beneath the eaves, to the darkness that greeted her when she closed her eyes in bed, it wishes upon the black-haired Titan before her:

If there are any wishes left to be granted, then may it be seeing Eren once again.

And having wished this, the something returns to its right and proper place—leaving nothing behind whatsoever.

Wall Sina, Goodbye

《CAST》

Annie Leonhart Stohess District Military Police Branch
Moral Control Squadron Private

E.G. Stratmann Marleen Co. Chairman

Carly Stratmann E.G.'s daughter / Runaway

Wald Richter Town handyman

Lou Meade Wald's subordinate

Wayne Eisner Carly's boyfriend

Bartender Bartender for Bar Pit Lidors

Cockeyed Man Regular at Bar Pit Lidors

Half-pints Regulars at Bar Pit Lidors

Hitch Dreyse Annie's colleague / Roommate

Marlowe Freudenberg Annie's colleague

1

Annie awoke to the sound of birds chirping outside her window. She idly listened to their tweeting. There was a pleasant air to it as if children were discussing what they might play at next. The room was not hot, nor was it cold. The refreshing morning air felt good. On top of that, Annie was off duty today. There was no boring ward patrol, nor eternally recurring paperwork, nor other routine tasks she couldn't understand why she was performing at all. It was an almost perfect morning and an almost perfect wake-up.

However, the thought of tomorrow's rapidly approaching mission came to mind, and she felt depressed. She let out a sigh. She considered just wrapping herself back in her sheets again, but her feelings were unsettled, and she simply could not get in the mood for that. In the end, Annie got out of bed trailing her gloomy mood.

Stifling a yawn, Annie took off her pajamas. She pulled on a long sleeves hooded shirt and put her uniform on over it. Annie did not own any civilian clothes. She did not particularly want any, and believed that she had no need for them. As long as she had several long sleeves hooded shirts, that was enough. And in her closet, indeed, several long sleeves hooded shirts were tucked away.

Annie made her bed. She placed her folded pajamas near her pillow. There was already no sign of Hitch on the top bed. She'd probably gone to take a shower. Only on off-duty days, Hitch woke up earlier than Annie.

Annie left the room and walked down the hall. She entered the washroom, brushed her teeth, and washed her face with cold water. She dried her face with a brand-new towel and felt a bit better. Now that she felt better, she persuaded herself in the mirror: *What must be done, must be done no matter what.*

The Annie Leonhart in the mirror spoke: *That's right, it's just like you said. I must carry out tomorrow's mission. There exists no exception of any kind. There's no room for compromise, no reservations or conditions. And what must be done, must be done no matter what.*

However, Annie thought. *Until I accomplish that mission, just how many people must I kill?*

Suddenly, that doubt arose and dug up memories. She recalled the ghost of Ruth D. Kline.

One month ago in Trost District—corpses / blood / flies / rotten odor.

Right before her eyes was a woman's corpse. The body was twisted at a strange angle, and the face's top half was missing. Decomposition had started. Annie could see the woman's name sewn onto her coat—Ruth D. Kline. A classmate Annie had spent time with at the training camp for three years. She had not talked to her even once.

Well, it might have been the corpse of Mina Carolina. Perhaps

Wall Sina, Goodbye

it was the corpse of Hannah Diamont, or someone else she didn't even know by name. That could have been anyone's corpse. At any rate, Annie couldn't remember well. So many corpses and so many names had passed before her eyes.

Annie stopped in front of that someone. "I'm sorry"—when she realized, she had said that.

"No use apologizing now, hurry up and give her a memorial service," Reiner Braun had told her.

However, Annie could not move a step. In the end, Reiner loaded that corpse that no one knew into the cart. Together with many other corpses.

Her self inside the mirror stared out at her. Annie averted her gaze. She gathered her hair behind her and tied it with a string—much tighter than usual. She pushed the many ghosts to the back of her mind. She closed the lid, and turned the key. She thought of tomorrow's mission, and became depressed again.

Tomorrow's mission—the 57th Survey Corps Extramural Expedition, Eren Yeager's capture.

2

Annie sat down on the bed and waited for Hitch.

Military Police Brigade Barracks—a plain two-person room—a dump. Empty wine bottles / dust-covered mushy romance novels / flung-off uniforms, civilian clothes, socks, and underwear / moldy bread / dried-up fruit / rolled-up tissue paper. Those things were scattered about the room to the extent that there was no place left to stand in. They were all Hitch's things. Annie had lived here for a month; on the third day, the room was in this state. When Annie cleaned up, Hitch returned the room to a dump within a day and a half. After that happened twice, Annie gave up on restoring the room to a normal human living environment.

Hitch was slow to return. Her showers were long, especially the morning shower on off-duty days. She would dress up, board a boat with her girl friends, and head to the capital to have fun— shopping / gossiping over tea and sweets / dancing with boys at a dance hall. That was how Hitch spent her days off. Wall Sina style. Annie was even invited once. It was her first day off duty after entering the Military Police Brigade. For no reason in particular, she turned down the offer. There was no second invitation. After that, Annie spent her days off duty alone. In the morning, she went for walks in town. If she saw a long sleeves hooded shirt at a street booth, she picked it up. If she liked it, she paid for it. After her walk, she trained to keep her body in shape. In the afternoon, she read books quietly in the library room. A quiet, peaceful, calm day. Annie rather liked these off-duty days.

Hitch still wasn't back. That was fine. Annie waited patiently. She did not have anything to do in particular. There was nothing she had to do or wanted to do—other than get ahold of Hitch and ask her for a favor. Hitch probably wouldn't come back tonight until after Annie had gone to sleep. Annie had to get up tomorrow before dawn, so she needed to get ahold of Hitch this morning, no matter what.

The soft light of morning shone through the window. Dust danced in the light. Annie blew in that direction. The dust swirled. It danced madly, spinning round and round. Before long, it subsided. She repeated this many times over and gazed absentmindedly at the dust's dance.

Finally, Hitch returned. Drying her wet sand-colored hair with a towel. Clacking her sandals on the floor.

Annie broached the subject. "About tomorrow's ward patrol, could you tell them I'm out sick?"

Hitch sat down on the chair in front of the dresser. She moved her face near the mirror and started to check for pimples. "Sure, no problem. But why?"

"I have a bit of minor business to attend to."

Hitch started to brush her hair. "You should just take care of it today, then. It's our day off duty."

"I have to consider the other party's circumstances as well."

"Can't you talk with them and work something out?"

"We won't work out anything."

"Hmmm," Hitch said. "Then, you owe me a favor."

Wonderful. If I owe you one for that, then you owe me dozens of favors, Annie thought, but didn't say anything.

Of course, depending on that *minor business*, there may no longer be a need to return here. So there would be no need to make any debts with Hitch. However—not something Annie wanted to think about—if she failed, she would have to come back. If that happened, she would have been absent without official leave. Of course she would be asked for a reason. It would be easy to fabricate some nonsense story and get through it, but it would remain in her record. If the absence was due to illness, it would not enter her record. She'd already confirmed that. Hitch had used the same tactic before. Many superiors had used that same tactic before. There was no mention. She did not know about the other branches, but at least this Stohess District Branch didn't bother to record absences due to illness—that was already confirmed. An absence without official leave, however, would be a different story. The organization was a stickler when it came to such things. Absences without official leave firmly remained in your record, and if some kind of undesirable situation occurred in the future, that record might prove fatal. A sharp person might make something out of it. Like those guys from the Survey Corps.

Either way, she just had to avoid her true motives being investigated from that small tear. She needed to take the utmost care—

that was one of the most useful lessons Annie had learned in her life so far. If she abided by that rule, she would survive.

Hitch put down her hairbrush. She pulled out a piece of paper from the pocket of her Military Police Brigade coat flung on the floor. She handed it to Annie.

Annie unfolded it and had a look.

A woman's likeness—her features still retained innocence—small eyes / small nose / thin lips / wavy hair.

Under the likeness was rudimentary info—Carly Stratmann (no middle name). Born 830, age 20. Height: approx. 160 cm, weight: approx. 50 kg. Marleen Co. Chairman Elliot G. Stratmann's only daughter. Stohess District 328 Ringitt St.

"What's this?" asked Annie.

"She ran away from home, apparently."

Hitch changed into civilian clothes—from pink pajamas with frills to a pink dress with frills. She sat back down on the chair in front of the dresser. Next, she started her makeup.

"And?" asked Annie.

"About five days ago, this was pushed onto me by an old-timer who told me to 'go find her.'"

"And?"

"I really didn't appreciate it."

"And?"

"It's a boring mission, isn't it."

"And?"

"I wouldn't get anything out of it, would I."

"And?"

Wall Sina, Goodbye

"Hey, about that 'And?' response, can you cut it out? It's starting to feel like I'm being interviewed or interrogated."

"When I think of another expression someday," said Annie. "And?"

Hitch took a breath. "All right, fine then. And, you might not think it, but I'm fairly forgetful."

"And?"

"Before I forget, would you mind returning that favor from before?"

I see. The quid pro quo—search for that runaway daughter in place of Hitch.

"Well, if you can't find her, you can submit a report saying, 'I did not find her.' The old-timer also told me that."

But if you submit such a report, your performance evaluation will take a hit, Annie added to Hitch's words in her head. That couldn't be a welcome prospect for Hitch, who wanted to strengthen her position in the Military Police Brigade and use her authority to the fullest to work her own angle.

"*And?*" asked Hitch. She applied some rouge. "What kind of guy is he?"

"?"

"Your *minor business.* You're going to meet a guy, right? What kind of guy?"

"He's a fifteen-meter-class Titan," answered Annie.

"Huh," Hitch said, mildly surprised, "you can tell jokes. Not very funny, though."

Cafeteria—mostly empty. Most of the members off duty were still asleep. The ones who weren't had finished eating a long time ago and had commenced their duties. Marlowe was at the center table. He was systematically tearing pieces of cornbread and ferrying them to his mouth like a laconic old man. He was wearing his Military Police Brigade uniform. Relinquishing his day off, he was ready to work.

Annie sat down in her favorite seat near the window. She ate her dry, bland breakfast while gazing out at the empty courtyard. As she drank her post-meal tea, she unfolded the likeness of the runaway daughter.

In the precise way that Annie didn't need to ask Hitch for a favor, she did not have to search for the runaway girl. In fact, nothing would be out of sorts even if she didn't. If she wrote and submitted a report right now saying "I did not find her" like Hitch had proposed, there would not be any problems. Her performance evaluation taking a hit as a result made no difference to her.

Even so, Annie decided to go look for the runaway girl Carly Stratmann. It wasn't like she had anything else to do. Besides, doing something would keep her from thinking and getting depressed about tomorrow. It was probably impossible to find Carly S. in a single day, but if Annie could gain some kind of lead, she could give that to Hitch. With that, her debt would be repaid. And afterwards, she just had to say goodbye to this stupid world.

Annie put away her dishes and headed outside. The sun was strong; the temperature seemed to have risen suddenly without her noticing. The people walking down the street had taken off their

Wall Sina, Goodbye

coats.

Someone called to her from behind. It was Hitch. She had girl colleagues with her, each dressed up in her own particular fashion. They looked cool.

"About what we talked about, I'm counting on you," Hitch said and blew a kiss. Gossiping with the girls, she sauntered off toward the piers.

Annie headed in the opposite direction. She started to sweat just from walking a little bit. It looked like it was going to be a hot day, the first in a while.

3

The aging butler led Annie to the reception room and indicated a leather sofa. He nodded and left the room quietly. The heavy carpet completely soaked up his footsteps. The door closed silently.

It was all rather exceedingly courteous conduct. Only a person who had dedicated an overwhelmingly long time to someone else could possibly attain that level of decorum.

The Stratmann residence's reception room was spacious enough to accommodate five or six teams. The ceiling was tremendously high. It looked like a four-meter-class could walk around unimpeded. The room was dimly lit, noiseless, and a bit chilly. The warmth outside was being shut out.

There were dozens of portraits hanging on the walls. Depicted in every one was the same man and woman. Some of the paintings showed them separately, and others the two of them together.

The woman—the runaway girl, Carly Stratmann. Annie hadn't been able to tell from the black-and-white likeness, but the girl had pretty, red hair. She also had clear, green eyes.

The man—considering his age, probably the father, Elliot G. Stratmann. There was no other possibility. No one would display dozens of portraits of another man in his own house's reception

Wall Sina, Goodbye

room—unless he had a very complicated mental structure. True, someone who displayed dozens of portraits of himself couldn't be altogether right in the head, either. To judge from the portraits of him standing next to his daughter, Stratmann was quite tall. He had abundant silver hair and a mustache, and his stone-cold eyes gleamed gray.

There was not a single portrait of the mother.

In the only stretch free from portraits was a fireplace made of smooth stones. Above that, two terribly heavy-looking swords, clearly not intended for use, hung crossed. Right by the fireplace was an old-fashioned liquor cabinet, evidently an antique, with bottles of various shapes lined up in rows. In addition, a bookshelf, a cabinet, and a wardrobe in styles that Annie had never seen before—probably from the bygone era—stood mutely. Outside a large window more than twice her height spread a vast garden.

All of these seemed fairly odd to Annie. She just couldn't understand what use leather sofas, dozens of portraits, swords displayed above the fireplace, liquor, furniture from olden times and such served for the business of living. The large window wasn't bad at all, though. Nevertheless, the smell of decadence pervaded the room. It was the scent of something dying.

Annie sat on the sofa and waited for E.G. Stratmann. The sofa was awfully comfortable to sit on. For the first time in her life, Annie learned that such a notion as being *comfortable to sit on* existed in this world. Everything that she had sat on until then—be it the chair at her natal home where she sat at the dining table with her father, the seats provided at the training grounds or the Military

Police Brigade Branch Office cafeteria and lodgings, the benches on the boats, or the horse-drawn coaches, certainly the barracks bed she had sat on a little while ago—was made with no notion of *comfort*. Compared to them, the sofa had been produced with an entirely different purpose in mind. Annie had to wonder how people who spent their days routinely sitting on these things came out in the end.

As if in response to her doubts, the door opened abruptly and E.G. Stratmann entered the room. The moment he did, he set his eyes on Annie and spoke.

"Why is a complete stranger sitting on my sofa in my house without my permission?"

Annie stood up from the sofa. "My apologies. Private Annie Leonhart, Stohess District Military Police Branch Moral Control Squadron. I'm investigating your daughter's—"

Stratmann flitted his hands around and reined her in. "I know. I heard that from my butler."

Stratmann sat down heavily on the sofa across from Annie. Reaching for the copper box on top of the table, he picked out a cigarette and lit it with a match. He puffed out the match with the smoke he expelled and threw it into an ashtray made of green glass. He'd spent a lot of time to do only that much, during which he didn't glance at Annie even once.

Stratmann, a large man, was even more formidable than he appeared in the portraits. His body was wrapped up in a deep navy-blue business suit with a striped pattern. His physique, attire, and bearing were good; yet, he was somehow worn out. Some

Wall Sina, Goodbye

lethal weariness seemed to shroud his figure.

Stratmann blew some smoke at Annie. "How long do you plan on standing there? We can't even talk if you don't sit down."

Annie sat back down on the comfy leather sofa. Her thought: *This is how they come out.*

"All right. And?" asked Stratmann.

"I've come to inquire about the circumstances surrounding your daughter's disappearance."

"In other words, my daughter hasn't been found yet?"

"No, I'm sorry."

Stratmann blew out some more smoke. "Why hasn't she been found?"

"It's not that easy," Annie responded. She could not tell him that it was because no one had looked for her yet.

Stratmann glanced at Annie, cunningly, ready to dig up some info. "You've at least found some leads, right?"

"No."

"Not even one?"

"Not even one."

"I see. It seems I've been working too hard. I can't seem to understand what you're saying at all," Stratmann griped. He blew out smoke like he was annoyed. "Ten days have already passed since I submitted the missing person search request for my daughter. During that time, I've heard the state of the investigation from messengers several times. All of you always responded persistently with 'currently investigating.' However, you, who are supposed to be *currently investigating,* are telling me that you haven't found even a single lead. In other words, are you telling me that you are that incompetent?"

Annie was being unfairly maligned, but not so much as to be bothered by it. "You are free to think so."

"No, not really," Stratmann riposted. "You're lying. You don't think that at all. I can tell when someone is lying or not. Those are the tools of my trade. You haven't been performing a search for the past ten days. You're not incompetent. You're just neglectful like your friends. You have not done anything at all. Isn't that right?"

He was half right—the tools of his trade but barely earned a passing grade.

"It's just as you've said."

"Not so." Stratmann dropped some ash into the ashtray. "You're still lying. If you were really a neglectful person, you would never have come here. You could simply stick to the 'currently investigating' line. You people are able to do so with a cool face. Yet you suddenly appear before me on the tenth day and ask me to talk about my daughter. I don't understand that part. And I'm in no mood to leave something I don't understand at that."

Right on the other half, too—excellent tools of the trade—there was no need to lie to this man.

Annie told Stratmann the truth—his request for a search had been neglected for ten days. Via two people, the case had circled around to her this morning. No one had searched for his daughter's whereabouts yet.

Stratmann's expression did not alter one twitch. An ordinary person would have either erupted in a fit of anger or grieved. He was quite a man.

"So in other words, that makes you the only person who is looking for my daughter?"

"That's right."

"How many years have you been serving?"

"It's been one month."

Stratmann laughed as if he found this funny. "I've paid so much in taxes until now. An outrageous amount that someone like you can't even imagine. Seems that this is the poor treatment I get. My precious only daughter disappears, the request for an investigation goes neglected for ten days, and when I think that the investigation is finally starting, a greenhorn who joined a month ago gets sent in. Like I said, it seems that I've been working too hard. I have no clue what I should say."

"You could tell me right now to 'get out,'" advised Annie. "And if you have this much financial power, you could commission a private contractor to search for your daughter."

Stratmann shoved his cigarette into the ashtray. Smoke quietly rose up into the air. He looked at Annie through the smoke. "That's not a bad option. However, there are just two problems with that. First, private contractors are a group of swindlers. They use their heads only to steal money. Second, I believe my own eyes. Having an eye for people is one of the tools of my trade. You're a greenhorn, but I've decided that you are a person worth trusting."

Smoke was still rising up from the ashtray. Stratmann ground down the cigarette butt again. The smoke disappeared.

"In other words," said Annie, "have we finally sat down at the same table?"

"Sure, that conclusion is appropriate," Stratmann replied. "Please, find my daughter."

"That is my job."

Stratmann nodded. He stood up from the sofa and walked on the thick carpet to the liquor cabinet.

"Would you care to join me for a drink?"

"Drinking while on duty is prohibited."

Stratmann snorted. "Your superiors always come here to imbibe while on duty. I hear it is 'part of their ward patrol.'"

"There are those types of people."

"The Military Police Brigade consists of 'those types of people,' doesn't it."

Stratmann filled a stout, largish glass to the brim with liquor and then returned. It was a pure amber-colored drink. With one sip, two fingers of it vanished.

"So you came here to ask about the circumstances of my daughter's disappearance?"

Annie took her notebook out from her breast pocket. "Yes."

Stratmann lit a cigarette. "There is not much in the way of circumstances. There was something a couple days before I submitted the request for a search. My daughter did not show up for dinner that day. That was something that had never happened before. My daughter and I make it a point to have dinner together at least, regardless of how busy we both are. As long as we observe that, we do not meddle in each other's affairs. That is the rule between us. But that day, my daughter did not show up for dinner. That's it."

Wall Sina, Goodbye

"When was the last time you saw your daughter?"

"When we had dinner the day before."

"At that time, was there anything out of the ordinary with your daughter?"

Stratmann blew out some smoke. "As far as I could tell, no."

"What did you talk about with your daughter at that time?"

Stratmann put his mouth to the glass. Another two fingers vanished. "I can't recall. It was idle chatter."

"What did your daughter do that day?"

"I don't know."

"What sort of social circle does your daughter keep?"

"I don't know."

"Any places she frequents?"

"I don't know."

"What did your daughter do most days?"

"I don't know."

Annie raised her head from her notebook. "You really have no idea at all what your daughter usually did?"

"That's right." Stratmann drained the remaining liquor from the glass. "She returned to this town after she graduated from college in the capital three years ago, and hasn't done much since."

"What was the name of the college?"

"Einrich College."

"Her major?"

"Chemistry."

Annie wrote that down in her notebook. Einrich College—a college attended by the sons and daughters of the rich, nobility, and royalty.

"Look," Stratmann said, putting out his cigarette. "Like I mentioned, I make it a point not to meddle in my daughter's affairs at all. That's because I, myself, hate being meddled with more than anything. As long as my daughter meets me once a day for dinner, I don't care what else she does. Even if she were out all day before dinner, and then went out again after dinner."

"Did your daughter go out often?"

"That was just a manner of speaking. I don't know how it actually was."

Annie tapped her notebook with her pencil. She shifted her tactics. "You're the chairman of a trading company. You probably have a lot of enemies. And you are wealthy. Is there a possibility that your daughter is involved in some kind of case?"

Stratmann shook his head. "If you are suggesting kidnapping, I don't think that's it. There haven't been any demands."

She might be imprisoned by some kind of pervert, or perhaps was already dead and buried somewhere. Those were also possibilities, but Annie did not voice them. "So your daughter did go missing of her own will, and you can't think of any reason at all why she might have."

"That sounds about right."

"Did you have a good relationship with your daughter?"

Stratmann picked up his glass. He realized it was empty, and put it back on the table. "In other words, did my daughter get sick of me and run away? I wonder. That might be it, or it might not be it. I just don't know. But we've always lived together, the two of us, ever since her mother passed away. We cooperated with one another and got along well. Of course, it might be that only I thought so, and my daughter disagreed."

A thundering noise drowned out Stratmann's words. It was the sound of the door knocker installed at the front door. Someone was knocking it. It seemed that that someone was rather impatient. Annie and Stratmann kept their mouths shut and listened to that harsh noise. Before long, quiet returned—the butler must have attended to it.

Stratmann, remembering, went to pour fresh liquor.

Something moved in the corner of Annie's sight. She turned her gaze in that direction. Through the window she saw the garden, but also the back of a man crossing it and leaving the premises.

Stratmann returned carrying his refilled glass. With one sip, three fingers of it vanished. He exhaled a breath mixed with alcohol. He quietly shook his head before he spoke.

"I utterly fail to comprehend just what it was that my daughter was thinking."

"There probably is not a father alive who understands what his daughter is thinking," said Annie. Her heart ached a little after she did. Just a little, not enough to be bothered by it. She immediately put her feelings aside. "What type of cooperation was it?"

"Cooperation?"

"You cooperated with one another and got along well, yes? Specifically, what type of cooperation was that?"

Stratmann put a cigarette in his mouth. He failed at striking the match, and the stem broke. Cursing, he threw the ruined

match into the ashtray. He lit the cigarette with a new match. "I already told you. We don't meddle with each other. That, above all else, is how we *cooperate*."

A disconnect.

Something was off—there was a disconnect in what this man was saying / how he was saying it. It was just a slight disconnect, and hard to pinpoint. It was frustrating.

There was a knock at the door, and the butler entered.

Stratmann said, "What is it? I'm with a visitor."

The butler whispered to Stratmann, handed over a small folded piece of paper, and left quietly.

Stratmann opened the piece of paper and looked at it. He contemplated it for a minute, then crumpled it up and tucked it in his pocket. He returned his attention to Annie.

"By the way, why did you join the Military Police Brigade?"

Annie looked at Stratmann. "Why do you ask?"

"That's because members like you are rare," Stratmann stated. "From what I can tell, you don't seem to want to be like your seniors. On the other hand, you do not appear to be someone who is burning with ideals and striving at her job."

"I joined in order to lead a safe, comfortable life in the interior," said Annie. "I don't believe there's a need for any other reason."

Stratmann gazed steadily at Annie. It was as if his two gray eyes could not figure something out. "That's right. It's as you say."

This man must know that I'm lying, thought Annie. *Certainly. I am. But you are hiding something too.*

"You still have some questions, I'm sure?"

"No, that ought to do for now," replied Annie. "If I find out anything, I'll pay another visit."

Stratmann nodded and sipped a bit of liquor. His figure appeared even more exhausted than when she first saw him.

If I succeed at tomorrow's mission without getting any leads on Carly Stratmann, I'll most likely never meet this exhausted man again. If that happens, what will he think? Wondering, Annie left the reception room.

The butler was waiting when she exited. Like a superior hound dog, he led Annie and walked down the long hallway. When he reached the entrance hall, he opened the door for her. Impeccable courtesy, as expected.

Annie tried asking the butler, "Do you know what the young lady usually does?"

The butler courteously shook his head. "I am not permitted to intrude on the young lady's private life."

"I see," replied Annie. *I see, he even lies with courtesy.*

Annie passed through the front door, and it shut quietly behind her.

What now? No leads. No places to go check out. She hadn't taken one step from her starting point.

4

The records room was cramped and hot. The smell of old paper tickled her nose.

Annie had returned to the Military Police Brigade Branch Office. She intended to forage information relating to the Stratmanns. She doubted that there would be any relating to Carly Stratmann herself, but there might be something about her father, the chairman of a trading company. Any little thing would do. She needed a clue.

There were fifteen shelves lined up in the records room. Three were labeled "Personal Information." Annie looked for the "Q-Z" shelf. She pulled out a wooden box with documents in it and searched through them.

Stratmann, Carly—no record after all. A miss.

The father was a hit—there was a bound file.

Stratmann, Elliot Gurnberg. Born 804, age 46. Chairman of Marleen Co. Took on the position seven years ago, succeeding former chairman Hans Georg Dangelmayr after his sudden death. Not a subject of surveillance by the Military Police Brigade.

Additional personal info—moving to the "A-H" shelf—Dangelmayr, Hans Georg—another miss, info on deceased people was

LOST GIRLS

expunged.

Moving to another shelf—"Company Information"—Marleen Co.

She glanced over it. She summarized the info and copied it down in her notebook.

Company registration, 815. Mainly did business with merchants from Wall Maria. Purchased grains, handicrafts, local brews, etc., from Wall Maria, then wholesaled those items to retailers in Wall Sina. From Sina to Maria, the company transported products manufactured in the industrial city—and earned vast proceeds from the profit margin. A typical trading company.

In 845, however, Wall Maria was destroyed. Humanity abandoned Maria. Marleen Co. lost its business partners and its vast revenue base. Marleen Co. rolled downhill. It was forced to reduce its scale. Ultimately, the only remaining operation was Marleen Carriage, a transportation service (carrying customers to destinations via horse-drawn coaches) started in 832 in order to diversify the company.

Annie returned the bound file to the wooden box and put it back on the shelf. She sat down in the chair. She turned some thoughts over in her mind.

Marleen Co. is on the wane. There's no doubt of that. Yet E.G. Stratmann maintains a standard of living that couldn't be higher for this world—with only a transportation service. It's nearly impossible to believe. He might have some other source of income. Maybe I should request permission to inspect their tax records? No, that would take too long. Not a chance of it being issued today. Besides, it's doubtful that

134

will turn into a big lead.

Fine. Then she needed to turn her thoughts to the peculiar father and daughter.

First, Carly S.—majored in chemistry at Einrich College. With that educational background, it should have been easy for her to find a job. A specialized one earning a high wage, in fact. Three years after returning to Stohess District post-graduation, however, she wasn't doing anything at all.

And E.G. Stratmann—he didn't seem to care that his daughter wasn't working. Not only that, he claimed not to know what she did every day. He'd said it as though he didn't care to. Moreover, he even went to the trouble of establishing a mutual nonintervention rule between him and his daughter—on condition that they meet once a day for dinner.

A peculiar father and daughter.

No—maybe it isn't so peculiar. If I call that peculiar, then my father and I are plenty peculiar as well.

While she was still living in her hometown, Annie was with her father from morning until night. She was woken up every day before dawn and spent all her time practicing hand-to-hand combat until the sun set. There was not even one day off.

Her father was infatuated by an unrealistic ideal. Compelled by him, day after day, Annie continued kicking the rolled cloth, stuffed with cotton, wrapped around his leg. She continued kicking the post stuck straight in the ground. She continued kicking the sandbag that hung from a tree. Even when her legs swelled up, she continued kicking. Rest was not permitted.

Her father's belief that training would help Annie carry out her mission was as immovable as a boulder.

Carry out your mission, her father told her. *Completing your mission is the reason you were born into this world.*

While believing from the bottom of her heart that it was stupid, Annie could not oppose her father, who forced her to master pointless techniques. She could not oppose her father, who continued telling her to accomplish her mission.

Absolute obedience—that was the relationship between Annie and her father.

Every family took its respective form. In another's eyes, it appeared rather peculiar. That was probably the meaning of family.

Wait—

Wait a second.

Annie had a flash of understanding.

Carly S. wasn't working. In other words, she was living off of E.G.'s money. Yet E.G. had talked about his daughter as if she were an independent person, as if she enjoyed equal standing—that was the disconnect that Annie had felt in regards to E.G.

E.G. had said, "My daughter and I make it a point to have dinner together at least, regardless of how busy we both are. As long as we observe that, we do not meddle in each other's affairs. That is the rule between us."

He talked about her as if she were his partner. But what did that mean?

—Wait.

Wall Sina, Goodbye

Wait a second.

Annie had another flash of understanding.

She remembered—E.G. had said, "I don't care if she went out again after dinner."

. After that, he said he didn't know, but it was possible. If Carly S. did walk around at night, she might have been snagged at some point—look through the routine questioning records.

Annie stood up and searched the shelves. She found it right away—the "Routine Questioning Records."

She pulled a wooden box off the shelf—starting from 850—the amount wasn't overwhelming. She looked through each sheet of the routine questioning tabs—drunks / drug addicts / perverts / vagrants / degenerates / peeping toms / transvestites / prostitutes / male prostitutes / exhibitionists—Wall Sina's East Walled City was full of such types. But she found nothing—*whiff.*

She went back a year. 849—there was quite a lot. The records were packed tightly in two wooden boxes. Countless names passed in front of her eyes. Her eyes were getting tired. Her fingers were getting tired. Her brain was getting tired. There was nothing—*whiff.*

She went back further. 848—her eyes began to prick. There was hardly any feeling in the tips of her fingers. Her head was throbbing. More countless perverts / more countless drug addicts / more countless peeping toms—her throbbing head was spinning. She felt like she was going to throw up. A name passed by. She almost let it get away, but caught it—*hit.*

Carly S. had undergone a routine questioning—she had been

LOST GIRLS

found drunk and crouched down late at night in front of a bar.

Place: Pit Lidors—a bar open all night. 74 South Bergbach St.

No special remarks: name, age, address / just a line that she was escorted home.

5

Annie headed to Pit Lidors—four blocks south, and two west, of the Military Police Brigade Branch Office. From there, she went into a back street. The sun was high in the sky. Not even a slight breeze was blowing. The sunlight was piercing. Sweat poured out of her. It seemed it had gotten even hotter out.

74 South Bergbach Street—a two-story building made of stone. There were cracks running here and there in the sun-faded walls.

Annie pushed open the swing door and entered the bar.

The place reeked of the stuffy odor of alcohol. The interior was dimly lit. The door creaked behind her. When her eyes adjusted, she caught sight of three drunkards sitting at a table—two half-pints with rat-like faces and a large cockeyed man. The three of them seemed wise to who Annie was. The two half-pints whispered and poked each other with their elbows. The cockeyed man slowly slid something into his pants pocket.

A young man was imbibing at the left edge of the counter. He was looking at a pocket watch in his hand. On the right edge, an old man was muttering something as he drank. Behind the counter, the bartender was sitting on a chair and reading a book.

Annie walked up to the counter. The old man on the right noticed her and approached. Drunken red face / shirt covered in stains / pants full of holes. He smelled terrible. It was a stench like alcohol mixed with urine. He asked what the Military Police was doing in such a place.

Annie showed him her Military Police ID and Carly S.'s likeness. She attempted to ask him if he knew the girl. But the old man wasn't looking at her ID or the portrait. He was staring at the vicinity of Annie's nose. The old man's eyes were cloudy.

"Um," Annie tried calling to him. The old man let out a grand hiccup. Muttering something, he left the bar. Something about it raining tomorrow.

Annie briefly gazed at the creaking swinging door. She decided to forget about the old man. She pulled herself together and tapped the sticky counter with her finger.

The bartender looked at Annie and stood up. He was as lean as a skeleton.

Annie showed him her Military Police ID and Carly S.'s likeness. "Do you know this girl?"

"Nah, I don't recognize her," the bartender replied—too quickly.

The young man at the counter glanced at Annie.

Said the first half-pint at the table: "Looks like a rookie."

Said the second half-pint: "You just figure that out, blockhead?"

Said the cockeyed man: "Go home to papa, girly."

Annie took out a copper piece from her wallet and placed it

on the counter.

The bartender opened his mouth. "You can break out coin, but I don't know what I don't know."

"I'm just thirsty," replied Annie. "Limeade."

The cockeyed man asked, "And not papa's milk?"

The half-pints rolled about with laughter.

Annie ignored them. A peanut came whizzing by. She moved her head slightly. The peanut hit a liquor bottle on the shelf behind the counter.

The bartender placed a bottle of limeade on the counter. He took the copper piece and left the paper change. He sat back down and returned to his reading. The young man at the counter drained the remaining liquor from his wooden cup. He wiped his mouth and left.

Annie drank the limeade. It was lukewarm. She walked over to the table seats. She showed the three drunkards the likeness and asked them about it. The trio's eyes said they did know, and their mouths that they didn't.

"Hurry and go home so papa can console you, girly," the cockeyed man said. He touched Annie's rear.

Annie grabbed the arm and put her strength into it. The arm went limp. The cockeyed man let out a short shriek. She pressed his head into the bowl of peanuts and searched his pants pocket. The contents were a matter of three to five years imprisonment—five white pills wrapped up in a yellowish hand towel—coderoin—illegal substance.

Annie spoke. "Let's call this property all of you three's. Enjoy your prison life together."

The half-pints tried to flee.

"You can try running, but this man will tell me your identities with admirable honesty," warned Annie. "It'd be best if you sat back down."

The two half-pints looked at each other. They reluctantly returned to their seats. The four of them sat around the table.

Annie spoke. "I'm looking for Carly Stratmann upon request from her father. If you tell me what you know about Carly, it'll be like I didn't see anything here. Everyone can go home without any problems. You can go be consoled by papa or mama, your choice. Understood?"

The half-pints nodded deeply. The cockeyed man quickly pulled back the yellowish hand towel with his good hand. He washed the coderoin down with his liquor.

Annie faced the cockeyed man. "I asked if you understood."

The cockeyed man replied, "Yeah, I get it, you asshole."

Annie took out her notebook. "Talk."

The cockeyed man didn't say a word. The two half-pints talked—at first hesitantly, before long as if fighting to be first.

Carly Stratmann came here almost every night. She always bought drinks for the three of them. She treated the other drunks as well. Carly was surprisingly generous. When she got drunk, she danced various dances to match the out-of-tune singing of the drunkards. She danced the tumist. She danced the gilby too. She also did the tangy, the chimy, and the swimy. And everyone danced the wachushy together. Carly was cute. Carly was popular. Carly was kind. Everyone loved Carly. About ten days ago, though, she suddenly stopped showing up. No one had seen her since then. No one knew why she stopped coming, nor did they know where she might be right now.

Annie spoke. "Did you notice anything different the last time you saw Carly?"

The first half-pint took a drink. "She was angry."

The second half-pint also took a drink. "Yeah, that was the first time I saw Carly angry. Everyone was surprised."

Annie: "Why was she angry?"

The first half-pint indicated the cockeyed man with his chin. "It was his fault. Because this guy took cody in front of Carly."

Cody = coderoin.

The cockeyed man did not say a single word, maybe he was sulking. He was doing nothing but drinking liquor and dripping sweat—his dislocated arm probably hurt a great deal.

The first half-pint said, "But it's strange. We're always doing dexy or benjy but—"

The second half-pint nudged the first half-pint with his elbow.

Dexy = dexedrin / benjy = benzetol—both cheap, crude illegal drugs.

Annie exhaled. "I'm going to pretend I didn't hear that, so tell me the rest."

The first half-pint burped. His boozy breath lingered in the air. "If it was dexy or benjy, Carly only chided us. As in, 'you better quit.' But when she saw cody, she suddenly flared up like a raging fire."

The second half-pint also burped. His boozy breath lingered in the air. "Just when we thought she was angry, she fell silent and started drinking. No matter what we said to her, she wouldn't answer. It was like a funeral. And then, she left after midnight. We haven't seen her since."

Annie: "Do you know why she got upset when she saw coderoin?"

The two half-pints shook their heads.

Annie changed track. "Why did you lie about not knowing Carly?"

The first half-pint picked his nose. "I just forgot."

The second half-pint yawned. "Our forgetfulness worsens whenever we're dealing with the Military Police."

The first half-pint rolled up his snot and flung it away. "And besides, I assumed you were planning on arresting Carly—"

The second half-pint nudged him with his elbow again—harder than before. The first half-pint held his tongue.

Annie: "Why would you think that?"

The first half-pint took a sip. "Why? I wonder why."

The second half-pint also took a sip. "I wonder too."

Annie tapped the table. "You won't be able to go home at this rate."

The two half-pints looked at the cockeyed man for guidance. Annie also looked at the cockeyed man.

The cockeyed man opened his mouth like he had given up. "It's because we thought Carly was doing something dangerous. Her father is ruined. Everyone knows that. But Carly has quite a lot of money. No one knows why. Just that it isn't money she earns herself or receives from her father. Her dad doesn't have that kind of money."

Annie crossed her legs. She ran those points through her head.

Conclusion: Carly S. earned money through "something danger-ous."

Conjecture: E.G. Stratmann knows this—which explains the way E.G. talks about Carly S. Naturally, he couldn't tell me, a member of the Military Police, about it.

"And," the cockeyed man said. He took a sip and looked at the two half-pints. "Right?"

The half-pints also took a sip. "Yeah."

"And?" echoed Annie.

Cockeyed man: "And a guy who couldn't possibly be a law-abiding citizen was searching for Carly."

The first half-pint nibbled on a peanut. "Yeah, he didn't look like a proper member of society from any angle."

The second half-pint also nibbled on a peanut. "Of course, we pretended not to know anything."

The two of them chortled. Peanuts covered in saliva landed in front of Annie, but she pretended not to notice. Annie asked the cockeyed man, "What was he like?"

Cockeyed man: "He was wearing a fancy business suit and had a false eye in one of his eyes."

The second half-pint: "His pupil was red. If you see it, you'll know right away."

Annie: "About when was this?"

Wall Sina, Goodbye

The first half-pint: "About five days ago."

Annie made a record in her notebook. She rewound the conversation. "What was the dangerous thing?"

Cockeyed man: "Well, that I don't know."

Annie: "Understood. I'll submit a report stating that you've been selling illegal drugs to kids. Your prison term will most likely skyrocket."

The two half-pints howled. The cockeyed man bent over and spat and said, "Quit screwing with us. I really don't know."

Annie brought her face closer to the cockeyed man. "A little while ago, you told me you didn't know Carly. As it turns out, it wasn't that you didn't know, you'd only forgotten. You also forgot about the false-eyed man. Are you sure you haven't just forgotten about the dangerous thing that Carly was doing?"

"Nope! I really don't know."

"Maybe you'll remember something on the way to jail."

"You asshole!" The cockeyed man sent the peanut dish flying.

"They probably really don't know."

Annie turned around. It was the bartender. It looked like reading time was over; he had both hands on the counter.

"So could you please stop harassing them already? If they acted a bit ill-tempered, I think it's simply because the Military Police makes a habit of mistreating them."

"Have you remembered something as well?"

"I haven't forgotten anything. I just didn't want anything interrupting my reading. I was at a really interesting part," replied the bartender. "Besides, I don't know what it was Carly was doing.

She never said anything about it. Carly's boyfriend might know, though. Maybe she's with him right now."

"Name and address?"

"Wayne Eisner. He lives in an apartment building on South Aachen Avenue. I don't know the house number."

Annie took that down in her notebook. "Did you tell the false-eyed man about her boyfriend as well?"

The bartender shook his head. "I wasn't here that day. It was another guy's shift, and he doesn't know about Wayne."

Annie looked at the cockeyed man.

The cockeyed man fretted. "I-I didn't know either until just now."

The first half-pint took a gulp. "Damn, that bastard Wayne got lucky."

The second half-pint sighed. "What does she see in him anyway?"

Annie closed her notebook and got up. She approached the cockeyed man, who flinched. She reset his disjointed, limp arm. The cockeyed man let out another short shriek. Annie stacked three copper coins on the table. "Sorry for the trouble."

The three men were flabbergasted.

Annie opened the swing door. She stopped. She asked the bartender, "Why do you know?"

"About what?"

"About Carly and Wayne."

"When you do this job long enough, you learn all sorts of things," responded the bartender. "Even things you'd rather not."

6

Annie left the bar. She breathed in lungfuls of fresh air. The sun was beginning to sink, but it was still hot. Hot enough to roast.

She decided to have a meal before going to Wayne Eisner's place. She bought a vegetable sandwich, rye bread, and cherryade from a street stall, then headed to a plaza. She sat down in the shade of a tree, where she relieved her throat with the cool cherryade and chomped on the sandwich.

Children were playing in the plaza. They went in the fountain and bathed in it. They shouted ambiguous words in loud voices, and roared with laughter. Mothers wearing hats of various shapes and colors exchanged gossip occasionally. Wiping away the incessant flow of sweat with their handkerchiefs, they squinted their eyes against the setting sun and gazed at the children.

A cat edged up to Annie. It was an old brown-and-white cat. She broke off a piece of the rye bread to share, and it was gobbled up in the blink of an eye. The cat flopped over and started licking its belly. Annie extended her hand and tried to pet its head.

The cat quickly rolled upright and moved away from Annie. It put some distance between itself and Annie. Then it started licking its belly again.

LOST GIRLS

Annie drank the cherryade. *Sheesh. Just what the hell am I doing here?*

"I'm not dumb enough to be amused pretending to be a soldier in this stupid world."

During her time as a cadet, Annie had said that to Eren Yeager. She'd meant it. The words had come from her heart. She had really thought so back then. She still did.

Yet now, she was "pretending to be a soldier" for some reason. She was "pretending to be a soldier" of her own volition. She was trying to track down Carly S. Complained and lied to by various people, her rear felt up by a drunkard, her legs stiff from walking around in the sweltering heat, wasting her time off duty when she needed to be resting for the coming day, she was trying to track down Carly S. Moreover, the case was starting to smell foul, unsafe. Yet she was choosing to step in it.

If she were asked why, she could only shrug.

Maybe it was because she'd seen the ruined, weary E.G. Stratmann. Maybe it was to avoid thinking about the coming day's depressing mission. Maybe it was neither of those things. She didn't know. *I don't know anything.* Well, maybe it wasn't just now. There were so many things she'd never understood. Was there even a single thing in her life so far that she understood? Nothing. Zero. *My life is full of things I don't understand. "Things I don't understand" are the main component of my life.*

She had trained in hand-to-hand combat without knowing why, from before she had any sense of self, and was sent *here* without knowing why. She tried to complete her mission without knowing what it really meant. Many deaths resulted.

I brought death to Ruth D. Kline. It wasn't only Ruth. Also to Mina Carolina, Franz Kefka, Hannah Diamont, Nac Tius, Mylius Zeramuski, and Thomas Wagner. Marco Bott—to him, too. She had brought death, as well, to a multitude of soldiers whose names she did not know. *And tomorrow, no doubt, I will bring death to even more people, and stain these hands with even more blood.*

And, the mission complete, she would return to her hometown and be lauded, bewilderingly, by a bewildering gaggle of people. Or maybe she wouldn't be lauded by anyone. She didn't care. In any case, once again, she would live a life full of things she didn't understand. *Along with the ghosts of the people I brought death to.*

Sheesh, thought Annie. *Enough for now. Stop thinking about all that. Something's wrong with you today. Just a bit nervous because of tomorrow's mission?*

Maybe that was it. Maybe it wasn't.

Whatever. If she didn't find any leads after visiting Carly S.'s boyfriend's place, she'd call it quits. She would head back to the barracks, get a good rest, and leave the follow-up to Hitch. Maybe tell her to get someone to assist her. Some serious guy. Like Marlowe. Marlowe would be happy to help. *Hitch might not like it, but that's not my problem. In any case, I can't let this kind of thing mess up tomorrow's mission.*

She returned her gaze to the plaza. It was empty. The children, the mothers, and the cat all seemed to have gone somewhere. Maybe they'd gone home. Maybe they'd just gone someplace else.

LOST GIRLS

Annie stood up. She left the plaza behind.

7

Annie made her way to a thoroughfare. She planned to pick up a Marleen Carriage coach. She might be able to glean some kind of information from the driver regarding the Stratmanns. She didn't spot a single Marleen Carriage coach, however.

Reluctantly, she picked up a different company's two-horse coach. She told the driver to head for South Aachen Avenue. The driver, who wore a deep green service cap, frowned conspicuously before whipping the horse.

Annie had never been to South Aachen Avenue, but she'd heard about the place. It was Stohess District's dump / a hangout for drifters / the end of the line. An area where migrant workers / low-income employees / the unemployed gathered seeking cheap housing. An area outside of the district patrol routes. The wall towered directly behind, and as a result, the sun only shone on the avenue for a short period each day. It was always gloomy and dank.

They turned right at Borchelt and got on South Aachen. The coach stopped.

Annie paid the driver. She asked if he would wait for her to return. It was impossible to pick up a coach here. If she walked to the town center, it would literally take all day.

LOST GIRLS

The driver shook his head—*Are you stupid, give me a break.*

Annie took a paper note from her wallet. The driver hesitated, then made up his mind. He raised three fingers. Hard bastard. Annie took out two more paper notes. The driver reached out his hand. Annie tore the paper notes and gave half to the driver—*I know what you're up to. You plan on taking the money and going on your merry way. You can have the rest of it after I come back.* The driver shrugged his shoulders.

Annie got out of the coach. She walked around looking for someone, but not a single soul was around. It was deathly silent, and that was eerie. Apartment buildings full of stains lined both sides of the street. An offensive smell assaulted her nose. There were piles of trash everywhere—rotten fruit / rotten vegetables / rotten unidentifiable things. A rat the size of a small dog was sticking its nose into a heap whose peak was a black cloud of flies. The stench of throw-up, urine, feces, body odor, alcohol, and trash mixed together and hung in the air. The smell was caked on everything. If she stayed here too long, she might catch some terrible disease. Annie sneezed. Her nose itched. Laughter came from somewhere. She headed in that direction.

There were four men in the back street. All of them shirtless, they were standing around an open fire and sweating profusely. They were grilling and eating something. It was probably best not to imagine what.

Annie walked towards the men. They noticed Annie and surrounded her. They were smirking.

Wall Sina, Goodbye

Annie asked the men—did they know a man named Wayne Eisner?

One took out a knife and scratched his neck with the edge of the blade. The other three laughed. All of their faces said that they knew him.

Annie spoke—lighting fires in the streets required permission, but if they answered her questions, she would overlook this infraction.

The man with the knife turned over the hem of Annie's shirt with his knife's edge. The three others wore vulgar smiles. Annie jumped away when they could see her navel. She kicked up the hand of the man holding the knife. It flew into the air. She sunk her fist into the pit of the man's stomach, then kicked upwards into his crotch. The man fell to his knees. The three others stepped back at once.

Annie moved over a little and seized the fallen knife. She stabbed the ground in front of the man's eyes. She asked again—did he know a man named Wayne Eisner?

225 South Aachen Avenue—a brown apartment building made of brick, three stories, three rooms on each floor, the middle room on the third floor—that was Wayne Eisner's lair.

Annie climbed up the stairs and knocked on the door. She waited. There was no response. She knocked again—stronger than before. She waited some more. No response again. She tried turning the knob—it turned. The door opened. She called to the apartment's interior—no response. She tried to sense her surroundings—

155

no signs of people—it was a go. Annie slipped into the apartment. She closed the door softly behind her.

She crossed the dusty kitchen and headed to the back room. Faint light entered from the solitary window. No one was here, after all. It was muggy. She was sweating just from standing there. She looked around the room. Bed / round table / two chairs / a built-in cupboard / a closet. She could hear light snoring in the neighboring apartment—thin walls, woefully cheap construction.

On top of the round table were a bottle of liquor, two glasses, and an ashtray filled with cigarette butts. Both glasses had been left half full—maybe he'd been with Carly. Maybe they had gone out. Maybe they would be back soon. Should she wait? No, Wayne might come back by himself. That could be troublesome.

Annie took out her pocket watch. She made a decision. She would investigate for just twenty minutes—swiftly / carefully / without making a sound.

She searched the cupboard. She pulled out the drawers—ink pot / feather pen / stationery. Bundles of paper / razors / syringes / indecent pictures. Candles / matches / spoons / pen knife. Some coins / a few books—nothing but junk. There was nothing like a lead.

She checked her pocket watch—seven minutes had passed. She had to hurry, not make a sound, leave the neighbor blissfully asleep.

She opened the closet. A sour smell wafted out. She scowled. A heap of dirty clothes and underwear. All men's. She'd have loved not to touch them but couldn't indulge her preferences. If she only had some gloves—but she didn't have time to look for any. She started tearing down the pile. She took one piece at a time and pulled it out, checking to see if anything was hidden inside. Sweat got in her eye. She wiped it away. She was half done. Nothing. Wasted effort. A sigh.

She checked her pocket watch—just a bit more than five minutes left, make haste.

She reached out to the pile once more. She tore it down again. She grabbed, felt, pulled out.

Wait. Something had brushed against her hand. Something hard.

She waded through the pile. She dragged out an overcoat covered in mold. Hidden under it—three wooden boxes. She dragged them out onto the floor. She opened the lids. Contents—coderoin. A massive amount of white pills wrapped up in oil paper. Three boxes of it—the street price was unfathomable.

Was Wayne Eisner a coderoin dealer? Was Carly S. helping him? Was that the "dangerous thing" she was up to? Then why did Carly get furious upon seeing coderoin at the bar? And why did she disappear? Why was the false-eyed man looking for Carly?

Annie felt someone's eyes on her back—she turned around startled. No one was there. There was just the bed. But she couldn't shake the uncomfortable feeling. The edge of her vision caught the reason. She looked down. Beneath the bed. Something was there. She got closer, stooped down, and peered under. She met eyes with a man. She pulled back shuddering. Her back bumped against the round table and toppled it. The liquor bottle shattered. The two glasses did as well. The cigarette butts scattered. A clamorous noise—immediately followed by silence. She pricked her ears—perfect silence. She calmed her breathing. She peered under the bed once more. The man's eyes were opened wide. His mouth was slightly ajar. She moved a fragment of glass to it. *Shit—not fogging up.*

Someone pounded on the wall suddenly. Annie's heart froze. A man's muffled yell: "Hey, be quiet, what the hell are you doing?! I just told you to keep it down in there!"

She held her breath. She stared at the wall.

He pounded on it again—stronger than before / roughly / violently. Again he yelled. "Hey, say something! Apologize! Apologize like always! Hurry up!"

Annie continued holding her breath. Her heart beat faster. Her palms grew sweaty.

"Asshole, making fun of me!"

She could hear the neighbor moving in his room. She could hear his slow steps. The sound was moving—towards the entrance.

Yikes—

The door—I didn't lock it—yikes. She ran. She tore through the room. She passed through the kitchen. The doorknob turned, and the door started to open. Annie grabbed the doorknob, yanked back the door, and locked it.

The man pounded on the door. "Hey, open up!"

Annie took a step back. She stared at the door.

The man pounded on the door, and it heaved. "Open the hell up!"

Wall Sina, Goodbye

Annie stared at the door.

The man kicked the door, and it creaked. "Open up, you asshole! Show yourself!"

Annie stared at the door. Cold sweat ran down her back. Cold sweat ran down her armpit.

The man kicked the door, and it screamed. "Quit screwing around!"

Annie stared at the door—if it yielded, she would have to take out the man.

He knocked on the door, quietly. He said, quietly, "Next time I see you, you're dead."

The neighbor returned to his apartment.

Annie sighed. It was a fifteen-meter-class sigh.

8

Annie grabbed the dead body by the shoulder and dragged it out from under the bed—a young man. He had a wound on the right side of the back of his head. Blood clung to it. However, there wasn't that much. He hadn't bled to death. He must have been struck in the wrong spot. Poor guy.

She put two fingers on his neck. He didn't have a pulse. His skin was still a bit warm—not much time had passed since his demise. His neighbor had said as much—"I just told you." He was probably killed then.

She checked his belongings. Cigarettes / matches / comb. House key. Wallet—several slips of paper money / several coins / license to operate a horse carriage for business use—name: Wayne Eisner.

Annie listened carefully. The neighbor wasn't heading back to sleep. She could hear him wandering around restlessly. She could hear him cursing.

She sat in the chair. She looked at the dead body. She ran over her thoughts.

Next course of action—

Option one, reporting to a superior officer—without a doubt, she would have to undergo questioning. There was no telling how much time that'd take up. And as the first person to discover the body, she might be included in the investigation. That would make being *out sick* tomorrow impossible—rejected.

Option two, pretend not to have seen anything—Wayne's corpse would be found by someone before long. It was this hot. Worms were going to start dancing in no time. A rotten smell would start drifting soon. The next-door neighbor wouldn't let things lie then. He'd summon the manager or Military Police and have the door opened. Once the body was found, they would unearth her involvement pretty fast. She'd revealed her identity at that bar and shown her face. Naturally, she would be interrogated even more harshly than if she had reported in—rejected.

Option three, leave everything as is, lay low, and head out for tomorrow's mission—seemed to be the proper choice. But if she failed at her mission, she would have to return to the Military Police Brigade. Naturally, she would be held accountable for today's events. If she got unlucky, she could be thrown out of the brigade. She wouldn't be able to complete her mission—the worst possible outcome conceivable.

Annie sighed. A colossal-class sigh.

Sometimes there were days like this. Days when you got in a lot of trouble starting out from just a trivial matter. Today was a typical case. It was so finely representative of such days that you could put it in a frame and display it. It was definitely worthy of a colossal-class sigh.

Next course of action—

LOST GIRLS

Option four, find Carly S. I could act like I found her before coming here. I didn't come here—I had no reason to come here. Once everything is taken care of, I'll report Wayne Eisner's death anonymously—it's the only way. I have to do it. I have to make up my mind. I've managed to get through crap like this time and again, brilliantly, like no one else can. I should be able to today as well.

Annie listened carefully. Faint snoring—the neighbor had set out to the land of dreams once more.

She stood up. She closed Wayne Eisner's eyes and returned his belongings to his dead body. She only kept the key. She hid the dead body in the closet and made sure the untidy room was back the way it had been. Tough luck for the forensics team, but that was that.

Locking the front door, Annie left Wayne's lair behind.

9

She walked to where the horse coach was waiting. She turned her thoughts around in her mind. She spun them harder.

Had Wayne and Carly S. been there together? Did someone kill Wayne and then kidnap Carly S.? No—that didn't make sense. If so, the door would have been locked to delay the corpse's discovery. The neighbor had already complained. And there were no traces of a fight.

Carly S. hadn't been there? Was the killer's goal the coderoin? No—that didn't make sense, either. In that case, the offender would have retrieved the coderoin. It was in a place that was easy to find. There were no traces of the house being searched.

Carly S. killed Wayne? Hard to say—the possibility couldn't be denied.

At any rate, coderoin was at the center.

Annie reached back into her memories. A superior had gone over it during a lecture for new recruits.

Coderoin—a newfangled illegal drug that started appearing on the market about two years ago, in the capital. It flowed into Stohess District only recently. High priced, good quality, highly addictive.

LOST GIRLS

Assuming Wayne and Carly S. were coderoin dealers, how were they able to get that much? It was hard to believe they had that kind of money.

Countless ?'s—zero answers.

Annie got into the waiting coach. She handed over to the driver her half of the notes. He seemed nervous, and probably wanted to leave as soon as possible. She told him their destination—the Stratmann residence.

She would let E.G. know. She was going to tell him there was no longer a need to hide anything. She was going to tell him that his daughter was in a fix. Then he could fess up about the *dangerous thing* that his daughter was up to. She'd have to suss out Carly S.'s whereabouts that way.

The horse carriage hadn't departed yet. Annie called out to the driver. He had a very apologetic expression. A bad premonition—Annie tried to get out of the coach, but was pushed back on. A man climbed in. Another man came in from the other side too. He was carrying a dirty hempen sack. The driver got down from the coach. A third man went up to the seat.

The man who had climbed up first thrust a knife at Annie's side. Despite the heat, the man wore a brown suit and a fedora. His face was carved with many deep wrinkles, and his right eye was false. A false eye with a bright red pupil.

"Sorry it's so cramped in here," the false-eyed man said.

The young man sitting to the left tossed a copper coin to the driver. "What was the destination?"

The driver caught the copper piece. "Aye, the Stratmann

Wall Sina, Goodbye

residence."

The young man said, "We'll be back in about an hour."

The man sitting in the driver's seat whipped the horses. The coach took off. They headed north.

The false-eyed man took off his hat. He placed it atop the hand holding the knife. The young man took the handcuffs hanging from Annie's waist. He pulled her hands behind her and cuffed them. Tightly. He frisked her. The notebook seemed to catch his interest. He handed it to the false-eyed man. The false-eyed man put on a pair of glasses.

It seemed the young man was even more interested in Annie's ring. He tried it on several of his fingers. In the end, he slid it on his little finger. He looked at it wearing the ring and smirked. "Hey girly, I'm keeping this ring."

Annie recognized the young man—starchy black hair / deep blue stubble / yellowed shirt. There was no mistake. "You were at the bar earlier."

"You think?" the young man said.

"You were drinking at the counter. I couldn't forget that stupid face even if I wanted to."

The young man pulled a pistol out from the hempen sack he'd placed on the floor of the coach. He grabbed Annie's hair. He put the gun under her jaw and spoke into her ear. The stink of raw garbage assailed her. "Girly, know your place."

Flipping through the pages of the notebook, the false-eyed man said, "I'm always telling you, Lou, not to act so rough."

Lou clicked his tongue. He ran the muzzle down the nape of

165

Annie's neck. Then he returned it to the sack. He faced outwards and spat.

⸱ The false-eyed man closed the notebook. He took off his spectacles. "Seems you're very diligent."

"I have my reasons," replied Annie. "By the way, where are we heading?"

"The manufacturing district. I'll be hanging onto this," the false-eyed man stated. He put the notebook into his coat pocket. He said no more after that.

"The manufacturing district," repeated Annie.

The false-eyed man took out a cigarette from his inside pocket. He struck a match skillfully with one hand. He lit the cigarette and tossed the match. He puffed out smoke, which was blown away by the wind. "There's a huge waste disposal vat in the manufacturing district. All manner of things have sunk in there over the ages."

"They say everything that sinks in there melts down into pulp," Lou remarked, laughing *hee-hee-hee*.

"It seems like your brain has been there."

The false-eyed man snorted. Lou's face turned bright red, and he spat again.

"Anyway," Annie said, "it seems like I've angered you guys."

"We're not angry. We don't get angry," responded the false-eyed man. "It's just that you have gotten in the way of a little business we've been conducting."

"By searching for Carly Stratmann?" asked Annie. "Even if I can't look for her, I'm sure someone else will."

"You shouldn't lie," the false-eyed man said. He puffed out

Wall Sina, Goodbye

smoke. "I heard from Stratmann. He said that you're working alone."

"When I met with Stratmann, that was indeed the case," Annie told him. "But the circumstances have changed, and I've been reporting to a superior. I need to check in regularly. If I don't, the Military Police Brigade will make its move. They'll start looking for Carly and me."

"I wonder," the false-eyed man said. He puffed smoke, then dropped some ash. "You discovered Wayne's corpse. You must have. You spent enough time up there. And yet your destination wasn't the Military Police Brigade Branch Office. Why? You're in some predicament where you can't report poor young Wayne's death to your superior. In other words, I've determined that you are working alone after all. Perhaps my conclusion is mistaken. What you say might be correct. If what you say is correct, we'll be in a rather awkward position. Even so, I'm going to follow my hunch. Well, call it a wager."

"You shouldn't lie, girly," Lou said, laughing *hee-hee-hee*. He took out several pills of coderoin from his pocket, shoveled them into his mouth, and crunched them up. Pulling a bottle of liquor out of the hempen sack on the floor, he drew a gulp.

The false-eyed man breathed out smoke. "Lou, we're working."

"It's an easy job," Lou spat again and retorted.

The coach turned left and got on a thoroughfare brimming with people. Lights were starting to burn in the city. The gas lamps illuminated the passersby.

"So you know about *poor young Wayne* too," Annie pointed

out.

"Well, I was planning to wait for you in that room," the false-eyed man said. He flicked his cigarette. "Just to mention for our honor's sake, we were not the ones who killed Wayne. We don't use such vulgar methods."

"Sinking people in waste disposal vats is hardly refined."

"Beauty is in the eye of the beholder."

"Then who might have killed Wayne?"

"Beats me," answered the false-eyed man. "He was acting rather recklessly, and all manner of people might have done *that* to him."

The coach turned right and entered a back street. Annie looked at the townscape. She guessed—less than ten minutes left to the manufacturing district.

"Hey," said Annie, "before I go swimming in that vat, I have one request."

"Go ahead and tell me," urged the false-eyed man. "I don't know if I can grant it, though."

"I'd like your *refined* friend to return the ring he stole."

"I'm not going to do that," Lou said.

"Be quiet, Lou," the false-eyed man shut him down. "The ring?"

"My father gave me that when I left my hometown," Annie lied. "If I at least have that, I can sink peacefully."

The false-eyed man looked at Annie. He stared at her. The bright red false eye reflected the setting sun. He faced forward. "Give it back, Lou."

Wall Sina, Goodbye

"You don't say, Wald."

"Give it back."

Lou cursed. He took off the ring and tossed it. It landed on the floor of the coach. He laughed *hee-hee-hee*.

The false-eyed man spoke. "Lou, I thought I told you not to act so rough."

Lou cursed again and spat outside. Picking up the ring, he passed it to Annie's handcuffed hand. "There."

"Thanks," she said. She put the ring on her right hand's index finger. Apparently Lou hadn't noticed the contraption. His brains had melted after all. Thanks to that, though, she was ready now. She asked the false-eyed Wald, "So, where is Carly?"

He looked at Annie. He looked at her with a perplexed eye. There was some slight confusion in its depths. "You don't need to know."

"You found her, then."

"You don't need to know."

"Why were you looking for Carly?"

"You don't need to know."

"What's your relationship with Stratmann?"

"You don't need to know."

"What is your *business*? Something that involves coderoin?"

Wald took and wore the hat that was hiding the knife. He transferred the knife to his right hand. He grabbed Annie's hair with his left hand. "There's no need for you to know anything. It's about time you shut up."

The coach turned left and entered into a warehouse district.

Wall Sina, Goodbye

No one was around. It was dim. The place was hushed—an ideal location.

It was a gamble—theoretically possible. A Titan shift that was meant merely to tear off the handcuffs—Titan shifting only from the wrists forward. She had never done anything like it. But she ought to be able to.

Annie flipped the mechanism in her ring with her finger. Slowly / carefully / without making a sound. The blade popped out. "I want you to tell me where Carly is. If you don't tell me, I'll have to kill you."

Hee-hee-hee, laughed Lou. "It looks like this girl has lost her mind. Do it, Wald."

"I told you to be quiet," Wald raised his voice. He stared at Annie. He was thinking over something hard.

"I'm serious," Annie warned. "What are you going to do, mister?"

"This," Wald pressed the knife at the nape of Annie's neck.

A go—she cut the inside of the thumb with the blade.

There was a small explosion. The handcuffs sundered apart. The back end of the coach broke off. Fragments flew every which way. The roof blew off. The wheels fell off and rolled away. The horses reared up, surprised.

Annie was thrown to the ground. She rolled on the ground, came to a stop, and got up. Steam covered the surroundings. She pulled her hands out from the Titan hands, which started evaporating. She stepped out of the vapors. She ran her gaze around.

Wald was curled on the ground. He was coughing. Lou was

also on the ground. He wasn't moving. The man in the driver's seat sat on his rump. He had wet himself. The horses were dragging the wreckage of the coach and running away.

Annie walked to where Wald was. She crouched down. Wald's right hand was behind his back. Startled, she jumped away. Her jacket tore. The knife was clasped in his right hand. It looked like he hadn't let go of it. Quite a man.

Wald charged in, waving the knife around. Annie grabbed his hand. She clasped his jaw over the shoulder and kicked both his legs from behind. Wald spun in the air. He fell to the ground on his back. Annie kicked into his stomach and thrust the knife in front of Wald's eye.

"Where's Carly?"

Wald sighed deeply. "Can I have a smoke?"

"Suit yourself."

Wald moved the knife out of his face with a finger. He crawled along the ground and leaned on a warehouse wall. He took a cigarette from his inside pocket and held it in his mouth. He sighed again. He quietly shook his head. "You're a Titan. You suddenly came out of nowhere, and made a mess out of everything."

Annie didn't say anything.

Wald opened the matchbox. He took out a stick. He looked surprised.

Footsteps from her rear. Annie turned around—Lou. The pistol fired.

A hole opened in Annie's stomach. A hole opened in the wall of the warehouse behind Annie as well. She collapsed. Blood

Wall Sina, Goodbye

flowed out from the hole. Her stomach felt hot like it was on fire. The taste of blood spread in her mouth. Good grief. She closed her eyes. She focused all her nerves on repairing.

Lou's voice spoke. "Can you stand, Wald?"

Wald's voice spoke. "Somehow."

Lou's voice: "That's too bad. You should've stayed asleep."

Annie could hear a bullet being loaded into the pistol.

Wald's voice: "Lou."

Lou's voice: "Don't worry, I'll carry on the business without a hitch."

Annie heard a voice laughing *hee-hee-hee*.

Wald's sigh: "You killed young Wayne, didn't you."

Lou's voice: "What are you talking about."

Annie heard the gun cock.

Wald's sigh: "Why did I ever pick up a ruffian like—"

Bang.

Lou's voice: "You're past your prime, Wald. You were always saying how tired you were. You said you were going to retire once you finished this business. It may be a bit early, but well, rest easy. All refined-like."

Annie heard a voice laughing *hee-hee-hee*. Lou walked away. Lou came back. He wrenched the ring from Annie's finger. He said something about a blade. She heard clicking noises. He said it was a nifty ring.

Lou's voice: "Girly, I'm taking this back."

She heard a voice laughing *hee-hee-hee* again. Receding footsteps. The man who had taken the driver's seat let out a short cry.

Bang.

The footsteps receded further and further and became inaudible.

Annie heard Wald sighing. It was the biggest sigh that she had heard up until this moment.

The blood stopped flowing. It might still take some time before the hole healed over, but she felt like she could move. She opened her eyes and got up. She spat out the blood pooled in her mouth.

Wald was gut-shot. Fresh blood dyed his pure white shirt. A slow death awaited him.

He looked at Annie with a surprised expression. He attempted to say something. Then stopped. He loosened his necktie. He unbuttoned his shirt. He was sweating profusely.

"Where's Carly?" asked Annie.

"At my office," replied Wald. "197 Van Gelder Street, second floor."

"Who are you guys, and what were you doing?"

"We're just handymen. We were hired by Stratmann a few days ago. He asked us to look for his daughter. He said the Military Police Brigade wasn't making any progress."

Wald tucked his hand into his inner pocket. He pulled out a flask bottle and opened the stopper with a quivering hand. He took a drink, and coughed violently. Alcohol splattered. Blood splattered. He opened his mouth again. He spoke—intermittently / coughing / boozing.

Wald and Lou had been hired by E.G. Stratmann. They had

Wall Sina, Goodbye

looked for Carly S. They got to Wayne quickly. Wayne knew Carly's whereabouts. He knew her secret, too. He told them he'd tell them both if they helped him out with a certain job in exchange. An extortion scheme—blackmail Stratmann with the dirt on Carly. Nab a ransom for Carly while they were at it. They were going to make Stratmann spit out everything he owned. Wald and Lou were onboard. They locked up the daughter and extorted the father.

"We were supposed to exchange the girl for the money two days from now," Wald said.

Stratmann—*Private contractors are a group of swindlers. They use their heads only to steal money.* Indeed.

"What's the girl's secret?"

The question didn't seem to reach Wald's ears. His vacant gaze was wandering about. Like it was chasing something Annie couldn't see, almost. "Just a little farther, and a boatload of money would have fallen into my hands. I was planning on saying farewell to this town."

"If only I hadn't shown up," Annie said, like she had no choice.

Wald snorted. His hand crawled for a cigarette that had fallen on the ground—but couldn't reach it. Annie picked it up for him. She put it in his mouth. She struck a match and lit the cigarette for him.

"It's not your fault," Wald said. He breathed in the smoke. With all his strength. He coughed violently again, and splattered blood again. He carried the flask bottle up to his mouth. "That's who I am. I try to grasp something. Just one more step. Just a little more. Then something gets in the way. The thing I'd almost grasped slips from my hand. It happened five years ago too. That's who I am. It's not your fault."

Annie didn't say anything.

Wald's gaze wandered again, then acquired Annie. "What was that you did? I should be asking you who *you* are."

"You said it. That I'm a Titan."

"That was figurative."

"Of course."

Wald snorted. "Even so, it sure was hot today. It's finally getting cool out."

Wald smoked his cigarette. He expelled a sigh along with the smoke. It was his last sigh.

Annie closed Wald's eye. The right eye—the false one—she left alone. She didn't know why. Even after having lost its master, the bright red false eye seemed to be gazing at something. Something that Annie could not see. Something that had not been named yet.

Annie took back her notebook. She could hear many voices. They were coming closer—probably having heard the gunshots. Annie made herself scarce before she could be spotted.

10

She came out to a thoroughfare. She hailed a coach and told the driver her destination. He seemed shocked by Annie's bloodstained uniform but didn't say anything.

197 Van Gelder St.—a gray three-story building. It looked manifestly shabby.

She got off the coach past the building. She could see the dazzling lights of downtown in the east. This place was dim. The gas lamps faintly illuminated the dark night street.

Annie hid in the shadow of a building across the street. She could surveil the office of the false-eyed man from there. A light on the second floor—she could see several men. They were being boisterous, making a racket.

Having come this far, perhaps the smart thing to do was to call for reinforcements. All that remained was to secure Carly S.'s person. Annie could make it seem like she'd reached here without having visited Wayne Eisner's apartment.

No—she would hold off on that until everything was over—she needed to proceed with the utmost caution.

Annie took out her pocket watch. She'd wait—until those guys were drunk.

LOST GIRLS

Time passed slowly. People passed the street in front of her sometimes. A young man with three dancers / a middle-aged man with a male prostitute / fat prostitutes shaking their hips as they walked. An old man swathed in rags approached, dragging one of his legs. Since he asked for money, she gave him a copper coin. It was her last. Shedding what she had served her fine. Three four-horse coaches dashed towards downtown. Young people were riding in each one. A young woman holding a liquor bottle was leaning out and shouting something. A band was riding in the last coach. The percussion was clamoring, the brass instrument wailing. The three coaches ran off in the blink of an eye. The silence returned once more.

Even though it was night, it was still hot. Everything was infused with heat. There wasn't even a slight breeze.

Annie felt woozy. She had lost too much blood. She was tired, exhausted. She'd been running around since morning. She stretched and loosened up her body, did some warmup exercises and loosened up all her muscles. The hole opened up by Lou had healed over.

All of a sudden, the window glass of the false-eyed man's office shattered. A bottle came crashing down. It hit the ground and shattered too. She could hear someone guffawing, someone else complaining. The guffawing grew louder.

Okay, go—crossing the street, Annie entered the building and climbed the stairs. The clamor grew louder.

A hallway opened up before her, and she walked down it. A door—the wooden label on it read "Wald Richter Detective

Wall Sina, Goodbye

Agency."

She knocked on the door—gently.

The room fell silent.

She paused briefly, then knocked on the door again—even more gently.

Someone approached the door. It opened. A man with a bright red face peeked out.

Annie drove her fist into the man's face. His nose snapped, and blood spouted out. She stepped into the room. She kicked upwards into his groin, crushing something. She grabbed his hair and slammed his head into the doorpost. Blood splattered.

She looked around the room. Lou was there. Three other men were there. They were drunk, and no one understood what had just happened. A once-tidy room had been hopelessly laid to waste—with liquor, food, illegal drugs, and incomprehensible sundries. The spectacle would have made the false-eyed man faint.

Lou shouted something.

Annie moved faster than him. She kicked the first man on her left in the side of his head.

His eyes went white. He folded and went off to sleep.

Lou cursed. He took out his pistol. He dropped the bag with the bullets, and they dispersed, rolling in every direction. He cursed again.

The second man drew a knife.

For crying out loud—it seemed like all the guys in this town carried a knife.

With it in hand the second man charged in.

LOST GIRLS

Annie dodged at the last second. She drove her elbow into the man's face as she did. His teeth snapped. She grabbed his arm, gathered her strength, and broke it. The man let out a short cry. Blood and broken teeth flew out.

The third man swung a liquor bottle down on the back of Annie's head. The bottle broke, covering her in alcohol.

For a moment, she started to lose consciousness. However, she hung on.

The man faced her with the broken bottle.

Annie kicked him on the inside of his knee. He collapsed. She grabbed his hair and kneed the side of his head. He, too, went off to sleep.

Lou pointed the pistol at Annie. She threw the liquor bottle at him. It hit, and the pistol fired. It blew off part of Annie's ear.

Lou cursed. He tried to load the next bullet. His hands were shaking. He dropped the bullet, and it rolled away.

Annie approached Lou. She approached him slowly. The blood flowing from her ear ran down the nape of her neck. It tickled.

Lou cursed. He waved the pistol around wildly.

Annie snatched it from him. She drove her fist into Lou's face. She kicked him in his ankle and sent him rolling on the floor. Then she picked up one of the bullets scattered about the floor. She loaded it into the gun. Lou looked at Annie with frightened eyes. She grabbed his hair and thrust the gun into his mouth.

Lou was saying something, but she couldn't tell what. Probably—"please stop." She cocked the hammer. Lou said something again. Likely—"I'm begging you, please stop."

Wall Sina, Goodbye

Annie placed her finger on the trigger. Tears were spilling from Lou's eyes.

She brought her face close to Lou's and whispered. "Bang."

Lou let out a shriek and soiled himself. A woeful smell drifted in the air.

Annie whispered into Lou's ear, "I was never here. You guys just got drunk and had a fight. Understood?"

Lou nodded.

Annie whispered into his ear, "I never met you nor Wald in the first place. Understood?"

Lou nodded.

Annie whispered into his ear, "And if I find out that you talked about me even a little—"

Lou shook his head. He shook it many times.

Annie uncocked the hammer. Lou fainted. Annie disassembled the pistol and threw it away. She took the ring from Lou's pinky finger. She wiped it clean with the end of her jacket and put it away in her pocket.

"Is it over?"

Annie turned around, startled. She instinctively braced herself.

The door leading to the room in the back was open. A girl with flaming red hair stood leaning on the doorpost. She was smoking. She made a ring with the purple smoke. It was Carly Stratmann.

11

Carly S. picked out a tobacco leaf from her mouth and tossed it in the ashtray. She drank distilled liquor from a half-full glass. Then she spoke. "Wayne, he died?"

"Yes," replied Annie.

"Poor Wayne," Carly muttered, blowing out smoke.

The two of them were on the second floor of the bar Pit Lidors. They sat across from each other at a table by a window.

Annie had led Carly out of the false-eyed man's office and said, *Let's go home.* Carly had asked if Annie would like to have a drink with her first. The two of them had come to Pit Lidors.

The drunkards were happy to see Carly, who showered them with smiles in turn. She danced along to just one of their awkward songs. She danced the tangy. The bartender who was all skin and bones let them use the second floor.

Annie gave Carly an overview of everything. She excluded the parts that required a lengthy explanation. Carly listened silently, perpetually stirring her liquor and continuously smoking. She knew just about everything. She said she had heard it from Wayne. Everything but Wayne's death.

The room was cool. The windows on both sides of the room

had been left open. The wind passed through freely.

Carly gazed at the city lights she could see from the window. She made rings with smoke. They broke instantly when the wind hit them.

Annie drank lukewarm limeade. "What was your secret?"

"I don't plan on going to jail just yet," Carly said, gazing at the city lights.

Annie shook her head. "I don't care about anything else as long as you go back home. No matter what you are up to, I'm not going to arrest you. I'm just curious."

Carly looked at Annie. She blew smoke at Annie, and knocked ash into the ashtray. "Coderoin production."

"Coderoin production," parroted Annie, astonished. "You made that stuff?"

"That's right," said Carly. "I made that stuff."

Annie tugged at her memories. *Carly S.—Einrich College graduate / majored in chemistry.* Even so—

"Is that even possible?"

"As long as you have morphine," responded Carly. "In the western region of Wall Rose, there's a vast papafer field under the Military Police's jurisdiction. There, the producers refine morphine. They can extract morphine from the sap of the papafer. It passes through various people from there, and I managed to buy a portion of the morphine supplied to the Brigade."

Morphine—painkillers / an essential for soldiers. Almost useless for the Military Police, however.

"If you get that, you can produce coderoin with things you can

obtain legally," Carly said, and explained how to make the drug.

First, you mixed morphine and ammonia. Heat for a few minutes, then separate the fica fragments and SiCl. Upon confirming separation, heat water up to 77 degrees centigrade, then add nitric anacetic hydride. This part required the most precision. You couldn't botch the amount even by a small degree. As long as you added the proper amount, the ratio of the chemical compound dropped to the exact standard value. After that, you just needed to remove the impurities—

Annie interrupted, raising her hand. She didn't have the slightest idea what Carly was saying at all, but did get that she really had invented coderoin.

"So, you were selling that with Wayne Eisner?"

Carly shook her head. "Wayne was just one of several drug dealers. Papa was in control."

Annie, taken aback again, asked, "Mr. Stratmann?"

"Right," Carly said. "He transported it to the capital via Marleen Carriage's coaches. He hired people and had them act as passengers. When authorized commercial coaches pass through inspection points, the passengers get checked, but not the cargo."

I see. The father and daughter were partners in crime.

"But the story was that coderoin was a new drug flowing from the capital," Annie objected.

"Which makes sense," said Carly. "Whatever happened, we wouldn't sell it in this town. That was the condition I gave my father when I made coderoin. As long as he kept that promise, I would make just as much as he needed. That was the rule between the two of us."

"But Mr. Stratmann broke the rule. He started selling in this town, too."

"In the capital, wealthy people were the primary customers. They know how to have fun. They don't buy recklessly. But the people in this town are diffcrent. That's why."

"So you got furious when drunkards at a bar had coderoin."

Carly rubbed out her cigarette. "Yes. After that, I confronted Papa. He tried to convince me somehow. I realized it was time."

"And so you ran away. What happened after that?"

"I stayed with Wayne for a little while," Carly said, sipping her drink. "I meant to leave this town with him. But Wayne didn't want to go. He tried to talk me into going home. I didn't listen. Then those two appeared…and you know the rest, right?"

Annie nodded. She drank her limeade. "But how in the world did Wayne come up with his stupid idea to blackmail his girl-friend's father?"

"He wanted money," spat out Carly. She lit a fresh cigarette. "He wasn't keen on going to some unfamiliar town and living like paupers with me, that's all."

Carly said that and quietly shook her head. She blew smoke at the night sky. She continued her story.

Obsessed with his absurd and stupid plan, Wayne asked her to cooperate. Carly refused. She didn't intend to get her father involved. She tried to skip town alone, certain that Wayne's plan would fail without her, but he locked her up in Wald's office. Then, Wayne proceeded with his plan. But he got greedy. He enticed

Wall Sina, Goodbye

Lou, and the two of them tried to outwit Wald.

"But according to your story, Lou must have betrayed him as well," Carly said. "Poor Wayne."

Annie didn't say anything. She was thinking of something else.

Carly lit a fresh cigarette with the one she had been smoking. She poured fresh liquor into her glass and took a sip. "Could you pretend that you were unable to find me?"

Annie sighed. "You weren't planning on going home, were you?"

Carly blew smoke. She sipped her drink. She didn't say anything.

"If you don't go home, that'll put me in a really tight spot."

"I'm truly sorry about that," Carly said.

"But you aren't going home."

Carly shook her head.

Annie sighed once more—her millionth sigh. "Why did you make something like coderoin?"

Carly looked at the city lights. She blew smoke towards them. "Papa had lost everything. I was trying to get it back."

12

The Military Police Brigade Branch Office was silent. There were only people on guard duty around.

There was a memo on Annie's desk. It was a memo from Marlowe.

Ms. Annie Leonhart,

A moment ago, a Mr. Elliot G. Stratmann came to pay you a visit. He asked me to relay the following information:

A man known as Wayne Eisner who works for Marleen Co. told me something about my daughter. He said that two men were looking everywhere for her.

Wayne Eisner said that he is being targeted by the two men for coming into that info. Please meet him and hear his story.

Wayne Eisner's address is 225 South Aachen Avenue, Apt. 302.

Yours respectfully,
Stohess District Military Police Branch
Moral Control Squadron

Wall Sina, Goodbye

Private Marlowe Freudenberg
Military Personnel No. 954

Annie looked at the time the memo had been written. It was a little before her search of Wayne's apartment. Annie shoved the memo into her pocket. She forged a transportation pass to Wall Rose in the office.

She returned to her room and took off her bloodstained clothes. She put on a fresh long sleeves hooded shirt over her head and wore her spare uniform over it. Hitch still hadn't returned. The room was the same as when Annie had left in the morning. There was no place to stand, as usual. Even so, it felt a bit good to be back.

She returned to Pit Lidors.

Carly S. was drinking with the drunkards. She danced the wa-chushy. She said goodnight to the drunkards when she noticed Annie. The drunkards told her they'd see her tomorrow. The cock-eyed man and the two half-pints with rat-like faces were there. The three of them didn't notice Annie; they just couldn't take their eyes off of Carly. Carly smiled at the drunkards.

Annie and Carly left the bar and went around to the building's rear entrance. The bartender was waiting for them. He handed Carly a cloth bag. There was money inside. The bartender told her that there was hardly any left. Carly kissed his cheek and told him goodbye.

They left Pit Lidors behind. Carly told Annie that she had

been depositing most of the money she'd earned from coderoin with the bartender. She'd been treating the drunkards to booze with that money. She said the bartender didn't know what kind of money it was. Carly and the bartender were, in her words, "old friends."

Annie asked her why she was so kind to those drunkards. Carly smiled. She said she didn't know. She didn't know, but she added that maybe it was because they didn't know that you can never get something back again once you've lost it.

The two of them walked down the street in the night. They were headed for the wall. Neither of them said anything. Carly smoked a cigarette as she walked. When she finished, she flicked it away with a finger and relaxed her pace. Annie slowed her pace to match. The two of them ambled along, like snails crawling along the ground after the rain. The nighttime town was quiet.

From somewhere they heard a song. A man standing beside a gaslight softly strummed a stringed instrument and crooned. The pleasant string melody and the man's deep, husky voice rode the gentle breeze and reached Annie's ears.

Down and out
Late at night
Fumblin' and drowned
In the blaring town

Luck is finally gone
He is just a rackabones

LOST GIRLS

The only way to end this night
Get lost and step toward the hopeless Street No.3

Without being seen
Scrabbling the deep
Is it the gust of wind through the gloom
Sharpness has increased its speed

See, it's simple as breathing
Even with your eyes closed
Brink of the night
It is luring you
The desperate Street No.3

Carly tossed a copper piece into the stringed instrument case at the man's feet.

❖

Annie's stomach rumbled when they got near the wall. She blushed. That reminded her, she hadn't eaten anything since lunch.

Carly asked her to wait for a bit and went off someplace.

Annie sat down on a flowerbed and waited for Carly. Quite some time passed without her returning. *I wonder why Carly is leaving this town,* Annie asked herself. *Couldn't she just stop making coderoin?*

No—I'm sure not, Annie answered herself. *Carly probably doesn't*

Wall Sina, Goodbye

want to watch her father go under. She's afraid she'll start producing coderoin again if she sees it. Carly chose the people of this town over her own father. She chose those drunkards.

Annie, too, had rebelled against her father just once. She was kicking a rolled cloth stuffed with cotton wrapped around his leg. Annie suddenly felt fed up with it all. She was fed up with it from the core of her being. *What are you doing, don't rest,* her father said. Annie kicked him in the face. He fell to the ground. She kicked him while he was on the ground. She kicked him all over his body many, many times. As hard as she could.

Since then, her father walked with a limp. He was happy that Annie had gained that much offensive power. Her father intensified the regimen. He imposed even stricter training on Annie and told her that she could get even stronger. Annie never disobeyed her father again.

Carly returned holding a bottle of limeade and a paper bag. Her eyes were bright red. There were donuts in the paper bag. She sat down next to Annie, and Annie ate a donut. It was the first time she'd eaten something so sweet and delicious. Carly smoked a cigarette. She made several smoke rings.

After Annie had finished eating her second donut, Carly said with a sigh, as if she had finally remembered, "I'm the only one who knows how to produce coderoin." She pinched cigarette leaves from her mouth and got rid of them. "When I'm gone, it'll be the end for Papa."

"Probably," replied Annie.

Carly flicked away her cigarette. It drew a perfect arc as it flew off. Putting a fresh cigarette in her mouth, she struck the match with her thumbnail. Annie watched with fascination.

Carly noticed and held out a cigarette. "Would you like one?"

Annie shook her head. She ate a donut instead. The two of them didn't say anything until she'd finished eating the whole thing.

"All right, time to go," Carly said after flicking away yet another cigarette.

Annie handed her the travel pass that she had forged. Carly accepted it with a thank you. She didn't get up, though. She gazed at the travel pass in her hand for a while. Annie told her that she could also tear it up. Carly didn't say anything. She might have been giving some thought to what Annie just said, or she might have been thinking about something else entirely. After some time had passed, Carly folded the travel pass and thrust it into her pocket. She held her hand out to Annie. Annie grasped it. Carly smiled. Annie also tried to smile but couldn't pull it off very well.

Carly got down from the flowerbed and walked toward the wall. Before long, her figure had melted into the darkness.

Annie got down from the flowerbed as well. She had just one other thing left to do. If she didn't do it, she couldn't say goodbye to this stupid world.

13

"Do you think that my daughter will come home?" asked E.G. Stratmann. "That is to say, not right now, but at some point."

"I don't know," Annie said. "She might come home someday, or she might never. Even if she does, I think it will be a very long time."

Stratmann put a cigarette in his mouth and lit it. For the whole time that he smoked it, he didn't utter a word. He rubbed the cigarette out in the ashtray. "No, she probably won't come home again."

He stood up holding his empty glass and walked over to the liquor shelf.

The Stratmann residence's reception room smelled as decadent as before. It was a scent exuded by the furniture from ages past, the tremendously high ceiling, and the portraits that crowded the walls.

Annie told Stratmann everything. Just like she had told Carly S.

Wrapped in deep green nightwear, sitting deeply on a comfy leather sofa, continuously smoking, and perpetually stirring his liquor, Stratmann listened silently to Annie's story—just like his daughter had.

He came back with more liquor. He looked exhausted, completely worn out. He looked much older since just that morning.

He reached out for the copper box. He lit a fresh cigarette. He blew smoke. A sweet fragrance drifted in the air.

"That's a really nice smell," said Annie. "Is that a rare cigarette?"

He looked at Annie absentmindedly. Then he shifted his gaze to the cigarette in his hand. "That's quite discerning. This used to be made in Wall Maria, and now, I'm about the only one who can smoke them. The stockpile is running out. When it does, I'll never relish this again. Everything that is good is fading away."

Stratmann said that and laughed feebly.

Annie sighed. She hesitated, but in the end said, "You killed Wayne Eisner, didn't you?"

Stratmann made a very surprised face. "Don't be absurd. What evidence—"

"This morning, while I heard your story, your butler handed you a memo. Let's start there. I'm a little confused as well. I'd like to get it all sorted out," Annie said. "Everything I'm going to say from this point on is my imagination. It lies somewhere between 'probably' and 'possibly.'"

Annie paused for a moment. Stratmann didn't speak. Annie continued.

"The memo the butler handed you was from Wayne."

The memo that the butler handed to E.G. was from Wayne Eisner.

Wall Sina, Goodbye

Wayne was monitoring E.G. He saw Annie enter the estate. Wayne fretted when he learned that Annie—or rather, the Military Police Brigade—was on the case. He feared that the whole affair might come to light and thought it was time to act. He devised a plan— to rip the money off from E.G. ahead of schedule and skip town immediately. So he wrote a memo and handed it to the butler. The memo said—*I'll return the girl right away. Bring the cash to my apartment.*

After Annie had left, E.G. headed for Wayne's shabby apartment building. E.G. and Wayne had a drink and talked. What they discussed was a mystery, but it led to E.G. killing Wayne. They were yelled at by the neighbor. E.G. hid Wayne's corpse under the bed, then fled the scene.

After that, Wald Richter visited the Stratmann residence. That was because Lou saw Annie gathering info at the bar, which meant that the Military Police Brigade was on the move. Why was Lou at the bar? He must have had an appointment with Wayne.

Either way, Wald demanded an explanation from E.G., and E.G. told him that Annie was acting independently, and also that she was headed for Wayne's apartment. That was because E.G. needed to send Wald to Wayne's apartment—in order to settle everything.

Wald, however, had already figured out that Annie was headed there. Once she showed up at the bar, it wasn't hard to imagine that she'd arrive at Wayne. Wald had already sent Lou to Wayne's apartment and put him on lookout duty. That was why Wald mistakenly thought that Lou had killed Wayne in order to keep all the money for himself.

After Wald left, E.G. headed out for the Military Police Brigade Branch Office. E.G. did that to put into effect a plan that had occurred to him during Wald's visit to his residence.

It went as follows.

E.G. would pin Wayne's murder on the two handymen. He'd have Annie arrest the two of them. Then everything would be resolved. The codeoin issue would come to light, but that couldn't be helped. He could fix that with money. Most of the Military Police could be bought with money. He'd bribe them every month. He'd keep it up with the sweet smell. He couldn't care less about such a pittance.

However, Annie was absent, so E.G. left a message. He thought that when Annie saw the memo, she would assume that the "two men" were the culprits.

"It that all?" asked Stratmann. "Just like you said, that's nothing more than your imagination. It lies somewhere between 'probably' and 'possibly.'"

Annie picked up one of the cigarette butts from the ashtray. A little less than an inch from the mouth end, it had a red line around it. She threw the cigarette butt at Stratmann. It fell on his nightwear.

"There were cigarette butts in the ashtray at Wayne's place, too. They were the same as these," said Annie. "They're the ones that only you can smoke, right?"

Stratmann returned the cigarette butt to the ashtray. He wiped his hands off with a few slanted claps. "That's only circumstantial evidence."

"Of course," said Annie. "You may have only gone there to have a friendly drink with Wayne, to smoke a few cigarettes and talk. Then you might have handed over the money, told him good-bye, and parted ways without incident. After that, Lou might have killed Wayne. However, unless you'd killed Wayne, there was no need for you to leave such a message for me. There was no need, no matter which way you look at it. That's because you could have told me about Wayne from the outset instead."

Annie took out the folded memo from her breast pocket. She placed it on top of the table.

"You shouldn't have left this. If it wasn't for this—" Annie broke off there. She shook her head. "In any case, if the Military Police Brigade were to start an investigation for real, you know what the results would be."

Stratmann put a fresh cigarette in his mouth. He struck a match. His hand was shaking. He wasn't able to light the match. He cursed. He was finally able to light it with the third match. "It was an accident. That piece of trash had no intention of return-ing my daughter. He was trying to steal my money by getting me drunk—"

"I don't care about that," Annie said. "Could you please stop smoking, though?"

Stratmann didn't seem to understand the request. He looked puzzled. It was only after a little while that he finally took in what Annie had said. Regaining his dignity, he declared, "You have no

right to make demands of me. This is my home. I'll do as I please."

Annie bent forward. She snatched the cigarette out of Stratmann's hand. She put it in the liquor glass. The flame went out with a fizzle, and smoke rose from the glass.

"I've been breathing tobacco and alcohol all day since morning. Everybody that I met today drank and smoked. Otherwise, they were doing illegal drugs. Excluding Wayne. I've had my fill."

Stratmann stared at Annie. "What are you so upset about?"

"I'm not upset," responded Annie, annoyed. "I'm just tired. I'm just exhausted. Tomorrow—actually, it's already today—I have an important errand, and I have to wake up early. Before that, I have to get some proper sleep. So I want to finish this soon, that's all."

"I see," said Stratmann. He put some cigarettes into the case on top of the table. He thrust the case into his nightwear pocket. "I'm going to be smoking in my cell."

Annie shook her head. "I'm not taking you to a cell."

"Then where are we going?" asked Stratmann.

14

Wayne Eisner sank quietly into the liquid waste vat. The ripples spread out slowly. Annie and E.G. Stratmann watched the scene from the vat's rim.

After leaving the Stratmann residence, they had headed for Wayne's shabby apartment building in a Marleen Carriage horse-drawn coach, with Stratmann in the driver's seat and Annie riding shotgun.

They dragged Wayne out from the closet, which was stuffy with a horrible stench. They put the cigarette butts from the ashtray into a cloth bag. They rolled Wayne's corpse up in a sheet, carried it outside, and loaded it into the coach. They placed hempen sacks on top. Stratmann asked what Annie was going to do about the coderoin. She told him he could do what he wanted with it. Stratmann loaded the wooden boxes filled with codcroin into the luggage compartment.

The coach headed for the manufacturing district. They fastened bricks to Wayne's body and thrust the key and cigarette butts into his pockets.

Annie gazed at the liquid waste vat's surface, which shone ominously in the moonlight. The slowly spreading ripples settled slowly. Stratmann asked if it wasn't time to go. Annie replied that it was.

"Why would you do something like help me?" asked Stratmann, who was in the driver's seat, ten minutes or so after they'd put the manufacturing district behind.

"Don't get me wrong," replied Annie. "This was for my sake."

"However, as a result, you're aiding me."

"You've lost your daughter. You'll be losing your business, too. You'll lose everything again. And this time, no one will come to your rescue. Not for a second time."

Stratmann rolled Annie's words around in his head for a while, then laughed feebly. "No punishment worse than that."

The nighttime town was sound asleep. Only the coach running over the stone paving disturbed the silence. The wind felt good. Stratmann abruptly stopped the coach. An old dog that had lost much of its fur was crossing the street with a sluggish gait, dragging a leg. After traversing their path, it modestly disappeared down a back alley. Stratmann whipped the horse again.

Annie asked a question that popped into her mind. "Why did you always dine with your daughter?"

"To talk about business," Stratmann said. "Coderoin sales, consumer data, the production output going forward, those kinds of things. Bizarre, yes? A father and daughter going over their drug business every night. And you, what did you usually discuss with your father?"

"Trifles," replied Annie.

The conversations with her father were always the same—where to aim to damage your opponent in the most efficient manner / what order to strike in to neutralize your opponent in the most efficient manner / how to fight while surrounded by a large number of opponents. Her father would ask the questions, and Annie would answer. If she was correct, he would praise her. They kept up those conversations for years.

Stratmann stopped the coach in front of the Military Police Brigade Branch Office.

Annie got down from her seat. *So long,* she said. She walked off towards the barracks. Stratmann called out to her. She headed back to him.

Stratmann cleared his throat. He began to talk as if he had something very difficult to say. "Whenever you feel like, you can stop by the house. I'll get you something good to eat."

"Thank you very much," said Annie. "But I don't know if I can visit. I might be leaving this town."

"A transfer or something?"

"No, I might be able to return to my hometown," replied Annie. "That is, if I'm lucky."

"I see," Stratmann said with a deep sigh. And, as if he were putting a valuable liquor bottle back on its shelf with great care, he added, "Best wishes."

"To you as well, Mr. Stratmann."

"Good night."

"Good night, sir."

15

Falsified report—Carly Stratmann headed to the capital three days ago with her boyfriend Wayne Eisner. It is believed that they used forged travel passes. Therefore, their names are presumed not to be retained in the registry of entries. What manner of person forged the travel passes for the two of them, and what kind of aliases they used, are both unknown.

Annie left the report on her superior's desk. She returned to the barracks. Hitch was blissfully asleep. A pink ribbon with a knit woolen pink flower on it sat unceremoniously on Annie's desk. Nearby lay a pencil. It showed traces of use. Annie searched through the trashcan. She found a memo that had been crumpled up into a ball. In rounded characters that wriggled like a slug crawling around, it said:

"You're not really out looking for that runaway girl, are you? Oh well, what you do on your day off duty is none of my business.

"More importantly, if you are going to meet a guy, you should at least put this on, okay. Because all of humanity is utterly aghast at your lack of sex appeal. Not that it's any of my business. H.D."

Annie picked up the pink ribbon with the pink flower on it—outrageously girly taste. She opened her desk drawer and thrust the memo and ribbon into an unoccupied spot. Carrying a change of clothes, she headed out of the room.

She walked down the long hallway and went into the shower room. She cast off her clothes and untied the cord that held her hair up. She took a hot shower. She washed her hair carefully. She washed her body carefully as well. She washed away the stench of alcohol and tobacco that seemed to permeate her entire body. She washed away the blood and sweat.

Sprayed by the hot water, she thought about her duty *today*. She thought about the mission to be accomplished. She thought about her life which was full of things she didn't understand. She thought about the many ghosts. She thought about her father.

The hand-to-hand combat training started suddenly one morning.

Before she started training, her father told her—*What must be done, must be done no matter what.*

At every opportunity, her father told her—*Carry out your mission. Carrying out your mission is the reason you were born into this world.*

Her father didn't tell her, but she understood. Having Annie carry out her mission was her father's reason for being born into this world.

Her father kept saying—*You must carry out your mission. What must be done, must be done no matter what.*

On the day of her departure, however, her father said, kneeling in front of her and placing a hand on her small shoulder, "I was wrong. I won't ask you to forgive me, not after all that. Even if you

Wall Sina, Goodbye

make an enemy of everyone in this world, even when the rest of the world comes to resent you, your father at least will be on your side."

Implicit statements were included in those words—*If you're ever in danger, you may abandon everything. You may even abandon your mission.*

"So," continued her father, "promise me, promise that you will come back."

However, Annie understood—she could never return to her hometown without accomplishing her mission.

She twisted the faucet and shut off the shower. She made up her mind—*I don't care how many people I bring death to; I won't let anyone interfere. I'll crush anyone who gets in the way, no matter who. I'm going to return to my hometown, no matter what—that is what must be done. And that is the only thing that I know.*

Annie returned to her room. She looked at the clock. Though not much, there was still time to sleep. She crawled into her bed and wrapped herself up in her sheets. She closed her eyes. Tears came, almost. She bit her lip and suppressed them. A deep slumber visited her in time.

Lost Girls

"Annie, fall."

Mikasa said that and gently kicked the female Titan's forehead. Like someone wandering around an unfamiliar town who had unexpectedly run into an old friend, the female Titan looked a bit surprised. It was the first time that Mikasa saw that expression on Annie. As far as Mikasa could recall, Annie always looked like she was bored. Or perhaps, like she was bearing something stoically.

For her part, Annie could see Mikasa's usual expressionless face. She could also see a small scar on Mikasa's right cheek through a gap in her hair. *Since when has she had that scar?* the doubt popped into Annie's mind. The floating clouds in the sky she could see beyond Mikasa drifted along slowly. The sky faded away. By the time she noticed it, she was falling.

Many scenes crossed Annie's mind as she fell well more than a hundred feet to the ground. It was as if pieces of her memory that she'd unconsciously shut in the back of her mind until now were starting to overflow. Several of these scenes she had lost long ago, and some were yet to be lost.

Trampling on fresh snow before daybreak in the pouring snow, heading for hand-to-hand combat training with her father, wearing her hood snugly on boiling hot days and running along mountain trails while trickling huge drops of sweat, throwing pebbles into the stream by the riverside with a refreshing breeze blowing, practicing anti-personnel unarmed combat with her classmates on a peaceful afternoon, basking in the warm sunlight in a sparsely populated library room in the quiet early afternoon during the cold season and reading, listening to the stories her father told as she sipped herbal tea by the fireplace on rainy days... Those scenes floated by one by one, then disappeared.

This was one of those—one among the several lost long ago—that only momentarily coalesced in Annie's mind and vanished back into the deep darkness of the unconscious the next moment.

❖

That day, after anti-personnel unarmed combat training, Annie was peeling the skins off of potatoes in the kitchen. She took the angular, unshapely potatoes from the basket to her left, peeled them with a small knife, and put them in the basket to her right. She only had to repeat that until the potatoes piled high in the basket to the left were gone.

She could hear the shouts of trainees coming from the grounds. They were probably one or two classes behind her. She could also hear birds and insects chirping in the nearby forest. The afternoon sun poured in from the wide-open windows, and the cool breeze that occasionally blew into the room marked the end of the hot, hot season.

Because Annie always made it a point to get to work early

Lost Girls

when she had cooking duty (generally it was peeling vegetables), she was able to pass half an hour or so by herself before the others arrived.

In the kitchen with the afternoon sun pouring in, with no one else around, listening to the trainees, the birds, and the insects, Annie applied herself to peeling the potatoes, carrots, and onions. When her hands got tired, she looked out the window and gazed at the birds playing among the treetops. After she had gazed for a while, she returned to peeling. Annie liked these stretches.

It was around when Annie had finished peeling her seventh or eighth potato that Mikasa came into the kitchen.

The door opened abruptly, yet silently. Mikasa entered with a supple, feline movement. She surveyed the interior, and when she noticed Annie, she quietly shut the door with her hand behind her back.

Annie was slightly confused. As far as she knew, Mikasa wasn't on cooking duty. Today's roster included Sasha Blouse, Connie Springer, Mina Carolina, Thomas Wagner, and Marco Bott. Mikasa's name wasn't on the list. No mistake.

"What are you doing?" asked Mikasa.

"As you can see, I'm peeling potatoes," replied Annie. "I'm on cooking duty."

Mikasa glanced at the knife that Annie was holding. It seemed as if she was measuring up her opponent's fighting prowess.

Mikasa Ackerman—she performed all training courses with a nonchalant air and was constantly beating out the highest results.

However, she didn't have a sense of purpose like Eren Yeager wanting to kill the Titans, nor did she covet a posting with the Military Police Brigade like the other trainees. It didn't seem like she was here for some sort of mission like Annie, either. Within Mikasa was a purpose different from everyone else's—probably something modest on an entirely separate dimension from worldly gain and profit that was difficult for other people to understand.

That was the view of Mikasa that Annie had based on her observations so far. An astoundingly brilliant, yet thoroughly selfless girl. Precisely the kind of person who was the most troublesome if she ever became an enemy. Annie understood that from experience, so she made it a point to stay away from Mikasa. However, the opposite party—probably with some clear goal in mind—was accosting her. Annie decided that she should proceed cautiously.

"What's up?" she asked Mikasa. It required Annie maximum effort not to betray that she was feeling a bit nervous.

Instead of answering that question, Mikasa closed the window. The sounds of the trainees, birds, and insects faded away, the cool breeze was cut off, and the sunlight shining in dimmed. Mikasa didn't seem like she was especially bothered by any of that. She took out a ring from her coat pocket and raised it to her eye, as smoothly as if she were writing the first line of a letter to a trusted friend.

Annie, who recognized the ring that Mikasa was holding in her hand, transferred the knife to her left hand and slowly extended her right hand to her breast pocket. The button had come off, and the ring that was always in her pocket was gone.

Lost Girls

"I found this lying on the training grounds," Mikasa said, still holding the ring up in front of her eyes. "I think you dropped it during the unarmed combat training earlier."

"Yes, that's definitely mine," Annie confirmed. Then she held her hand out to Mikasa. "Thanks."

Instead of placing the ring in the palm of Annie's extended hand, Mikasa flicked the mechanism with her finger. It made a dry click, and a blade projected out from the ring. It looked even smaller and less reliable than usual.

"What's this?" asked Mikasa.

"A self-defense item," replied Annie.

Mikasa cast another glance at the blade jutting out from the ring before returning her gaze to Annie.

Perhaps Annie had replied too quickly.

"A self-defense item," Mikasa repeated after a brief pause. "You seem pretty proficient at anti-personnel unarmed combat. I don't see why you need this."

"There are situations that I can't handle with hand-to-hand combat skills alone."

"If the situation can't be handled with your hand-to-hand combat skills, I don't see how this would be useful."

Annie took a short breath, then looked at Mikasa. No semblance of an expression appeared on the girl's face, and Annie could not read any emotions from it. "What are you trying to say?"

"I'm not trying to say anything, nor do I want to hear any nonsense about 'self-defense,'" Mikasa said. "I'm just asking why, for what reason, you are carrying such a dangerous thing."

LOST GIRLS

Good grief, thought Annie, *speaking of situations that hand-to-hand combat alone can't handle. And those situations always demand the utmost caution. There is no such thing as being too cautious.*

"My father…my parents gave it to me when they sent me out from my hometown," lied Annie.

Mikasa didn't say anything and just stared at Annie, as if to tease out some kind of discrepancy in Annie's words. Then the girl cast another fleeting glance at the knife in Annie's hand.

Annie had been grasping the knife tightly despite herself. It felt like her fingers and the knife's handle had assimilated each other. She couldn't let go of the knife yet, though.

The trainees, birds, and insects were still faintly audible from outside the shut window. The sounds seemed to carry all this way from very far away.

"My parents are awful worrywarts," Annie added cautiously. "You get it, right? Because they were sending their daughter to an unfamiliar place, as parents, they wanted me to carry a self-defense item at least. Even if it won't serve any use. Aren't your parents the same way?"

"I have no parents," Mikasa said, concisely, as if she were reading aloud a sentence from a textbook. Her delivery lacked any and all emotion.

Recalling that Mikasa was from Shiganshina District, Annie's heart ached a little. She balked, but it wouldn't do not to ask. "Were they killed by the Titans?"

"Not by the Titans."

Annie waited for the rest of the story, but Mikasa held her

tongue. It was an eloquent silence that declared her lack of interest in continuing the story. From there, it wasn't difficult to surmise that some dark incident had befallen Mikasa.

"I see… I'm sorry, I was being rude," apologized Annie.

Mikasa quietly shook her head. Her beautiful black hair swayed like silk. Then, putting away the jutting blade, she presented the ring to Annie.

"Thanks," Annie said, accepting it. "And? Why are you so interested in this ring?"

"I just don't want you to be wearing such a dangerous ring when you go up against Eren during hand-to-hand combat training. If that blade popped out thanks to some kind of shock during practice, Eren might get hurt."

"Of course." Annie relaxed, trying not to be too obvious about it. *Of course that was it.* As though tearing off one finger at a time, she let go of the knife and placed it on the table. She ran her clammy palms against her pants to wipe off the sweat. "You can rest easy. Because this is more like a charm, I hardly ever put it on."

"That's fine then." Mikasa looked at the mountain of unpeeled potatoes piled in the basket. "Sorry for bothering you."

Then, proceeding to the door, she opened it. She didn't leave right away, however. Some slight suspicion in the back of her mind seemed to be holding her back. Before long, Mikasa turned to Annie and spoke.

"Why are you here?"

"I think I just told you. That I'm on cooking duty."

"No. I'm asking why you're here at the training grounds."

LOST GIRLS

Annie wrinkled her brow reflexively. It might have been too late, but she shrugged her shoulders to try to gloss over that. Further, she answered in her best cheerful voice—though not so cheerfully as to be overdoing it.

"I'm here for the same reason as the other guys. I just want to join the Military Police Brigade. I just want to live well in a safe, pleasant place. Though you seem different."

Mikasa focused directly on Annie, and the girl's eyes looked like they might see through to the other side of Annie's heart.

It was then that Annie finally realized. Mikasa had probably killed. Her deep, clear eyes belonged to someone who had ended a human life with her own hands. Annie knew several other people who had the same eyes.

"I somehow get that you want to join the Military Police Brigade," Mikasa said. "But I feel like it's not because you want to live well in a safe, pleasant place."

"Why not?"

"The others want to get away because they're afraid of the Titans. Or maybe they crave luxury."

"There was also someone who wanted to serve the king, life and soul."

"You aren't like any of them. I don't think."

"So why do I want to join the Military Police Brigade?"

"Because you have to," Mikasa stated. "I think."

Good grief, this is why I wanted to stay away from this girl. "You think too much of me," Annie said. "I really just want to live in luxury."

Lost Girls

"You look as if you've been putting up with something all along."

"Putting up," echoed Annie. "What am I putting up with?"

"Don't ask me."

Annie snorted and gently shook her head. "That's right. Point taken."

And then she looked out the window. The birds that had been playing merrily in the treetops just a little while ago were no longer there. Maybe they'd gone where they needed to go, maybe they'd returned to where they needed to return. The sun was much weaker than it was before; the signs of dusk imbued the air outside the window. A gentle breeze blew and shook the leaves.

"Annie, what's burdening you?"

Annie returned her gaze to Mikasa, then shrugged again. "We all have burdens to bear, right? Mine isn't so different from what the other guys are bearing."

Mikasa turned that over in her head for some time. She made to say something but swallowed her words as if she'd thought better of it.

"Hey, Mikasa," Annie said, tapping the table steadily with the ring, "this thing might be a trinket with no use, but it's not something that I can just throw away. I think that's what it is."

"Because you received it from your parents."

"Even excluding that circumstance," Annie said, and went on, not understanding herself why she was babbling about this. "Since the thing was created with some kind of purpose—even if it's a trivial purpose that no one cares for—I can't be callous about it.

That must be what's burdening me."

Mikasa looked at the ring in Annie's hand. "But it might be useful in situations that hand-to-hand combat alone can't handle."

"Right. It might be useful in situations that hand-to-hand combat alone can't handle."

"I hope those situations don't happen," Mikasa said with her usual expressionless face, in her usual voice devoid of emotion. Then she slipped out of the kitchen. With a supple movement just like when she had entered.

For some time after Mikasa had left, Annie gazed at the closed door. Orange rays poured in through the window and made pools of light on the floor between Annie and the door. She could no longer hear the trainees or birds' calls, only the insects' chirping.

I hope so too, Annie eventually muttered at the closed door. Perhaps it was only to herself. *Really, I hope that from the bottom of my heart. And yet*, thought Annie. *And yet*, that day *will come in time. Just as death catches up to you in time*, that day *will arrive, inevitably.*

Annie took a breath and put the ring into her breast pocket. Then, as if it had just occurred to her, she opened the window. A gentle breeze blew in and brushed her cheek. Annie hoped that it was a wind blowing from outside the wall. And that the arrival of *that day* was as far in the future as possible.

It was in 849, towards the end of a hot, hot season, on a certain afternoon when a gentle refreshing breeze blew, that the above event transpired between Annie and Mikasa.

Lost Girls

❖

"Annie, fall," Mikasa said. Then she gently kicked Annie's forehead.

Perhaps it needed to be Mikasa, and no one else. The thought occurred to Annie among her jumbled recollections as she looked up at the receding sky and fell well more than a hundred feet to the ground.